CHANGING HER HEART

GAIL SATTLER

Steeple
Hill®

Published by Steeple Hill Books™

STEEPLE HILL BOOKS

Steeple
Hill®

ISBN 0-373-87352-2

CHANGING HER HEART

www.SteepleHill.com

Printed in U.S.A.

Turn from evil and do good;
then you will dwell in the land forever.
—*Psalms* 37:27

Dedicated to my husband, Tim, and my kids Justin,
Chris and Tyrone, who take care of stuff so
I can write, no matter how long it takes
or how crazy things get.

Chapter One

"There's something you don't see very often."

Lacey Dachin's mouth dropped open. All the pins she'd had pressed between her lips fell to the floor.

A man was standing at the panty hose rack, holding two types of panty hose, one package in each hand, quite obviously comparison shopping.

Lacey got to her feet, knowing she would never get her customer's hem straight now.

She kept her voice down to a whisper. "You know, Vivian, I've seen him before, but I can't remember where."

Lacey and Vivian stared as the man looked back and forth between the two packages, and then appeared to study one of them more closely.

"The one he's so interested in is the most expensive we have," Lacey muttered.

He tucked the less-expensive package back into the rack, and continued reading.

Vivian's gaze dropped to the man's pants. "I hope he's not buying them for himself."

Lacey stiffened. As creepy as it was, she couldn't stand in judgment. "Who he's buying them for is not my concern. It is only my concern that he needs help."

"Then...then I think I should be going," Vivian stammered. "I'll leave the dress in the changing room, and I'll be back on Friday."

"Thanks. That gives me plenty of time. I'll see you then."

Once Vivian disappeared back into the changing room, Lacey gathered her courage and swallowed hard. She'd seen many odd things over the years when she worked at the La Boutique downtown branch, but this was not something she expected to deal with at the suburban outlet. "Can I help you?" she asked as she approached him.

"Um, yes.... Can you turn around for a minute?"

Lacey turned around. She didn't understand what it was he didn't want her to see, but again, she wasn't sure she really wanted to know.

"That's good. Thanks."

As she turned back to him, she saw his cheeks redden, and he averted his eyes. "I—I guess you're about the same height and, uh, stuff," he stammered, then extended the package toward her. "Without having to get too personal, what size would you buy if you were buying these for yourself?"

Lacey felt her own cheeks burn. The sizing on the back of the package was determined by height and weight. She had a bad feeling she knew what he had been looking at when she turned around, but at least he hadn't asked her to bend over. For a second she considered telling him one size lower than her own, but his reason for wanting to know had nothing to do with her vanity.

"I'd buy that size. Is it the right color?"

"I guess so. I'll take it."

She started walking toward the sales counter, not quite comfortable with him being behind her. "Is there anything else I can get for you?" she asked over her shoulder.

Once again, his cheeks darkened. "No," he mumbled. "I think this is enough torture for one day."

Feeling bolder with the counter between them, she finally noticed he was wearing the name badge, "Randy."

"You work at the computer store next door, don't you?"

The red blush crept upward to his ears. He stared down at the counter and pushed the package closer to her. "Yes."

"Can I ask you something?"

His lips tightened. "This isn't for me."

"Actually, I need to buy a computer, and I need help to figure out what kind."

His entire posture relaxed and he raised his head. "In that case, ask me anything," he said with a smile.

Lacey's breath caught at the sudden eye contact. It suddenly hit her what an attractive man he was. His blue eyes sparkled and little crinkles appeared at the sides of his eyes, making him almost movie-star handsome. Not that she had never come in contact with a good-looking man, but it was rare to find one in the hosiery section.

She returned her attention to the transaction. "I don't know much about computers."

"That doesn't matter. I can still help you pick the right one. Do you want a desktop or a laptop?"

"I don't really know. Bryce went back to university, and now he's in his last year. Everyone says his computer is too old to be upgraded, so I'm going to surprise him with a new one for his birthday."

His smile faltered, but only momentarily. "That's a really nice surprise. If you tell me how much you want to spend, I'll show you a few."

"I'd like that."

Randy checked his watch. "I'm sorry to do this, but I have to get back—my break is up. If you want to come into the store, I can show you anything you want to see."

"Thanks. I appreciate it."

He nodded, and before she could say any more, he turned and walked out.

Lacey stared at the empty space. She'd tried to make it a pleasant transaction, yet it appeared that he still felt awkward. But she really did need a computer, and for some reason, she trusted him, even if he did buy panty hose.

Randy Reynolds tossed the bag containing the panty hose onto the counter toward Carol. It skimmed past the cash register and came to a stop inches from her hand.

"I hope you're happy," he grumbled. "I've never been so embarrassed in my life."

"Knowing you, I doubt that," Carol said, then laughed, which only made Randy more annoyed. She lowered her head and began to pick at the hole in the panty hose on her leg. "Besides, this was your fault."

"It was *your* fault for standing too close and getting in the way. I told you to move when I was rearranging those display cases." He glared in disgust at the bag.

"Quit complaining and look on the bright side. This gave you a chance to meet Lacey. Isn't she cute?"

"She's a grown woman, not a six year old. She's not cute."

Carol leaned over the counter and latched on to his

sleeve, preventing him from walking away. "No. She's more than cute. She's gorgeous. And she's nice, too."

Randy stared down at Carol's perfectly manicured hand. "Forget it. I'm not interested."

Carol pulled his sleeve, forcing him closer. The only reason he complied was because he didn't want to make a scene while they were supposed to be working.

Her voice lowered to just barely above a whisper. "I don't understand you. Why don't you date women?"

"It's okay. I don't date men, either."

She failed to laugh at his little joke. Unfortunately, she also failed to release him. "You know what I mean. I want you to be happy."

"I'd be happy if you let me go."

She did, but instead of letting him get back to work, Carol hustled out from behind the counter and stood in front of him. "Look at me!"

Carol ran her fingers through her bright red hair, the color of which Randy knew came out of a bottle. He couldn't help but compare the fake color of Carol's hair to the natural brown of Lacey's. He liked the natural shade of Lacey's better.

"What about you?" he asked.

Carol raised her left hand and flashed her engagement ring in front of his nose. Not for the first time, the size caused him to wonder if the diamond was as fake as her hair.

"See how happy I am? I want you to be happy, too. My wedding is only two hundred and twenty-seven days away."

And his best friend Bob's wedding to Georgette was getting closer, as well.

At the thought of Bob's upcoming wedding, Randy's heart clenched. Bob was getting married, and their friend Adrian was married. Already Celeste was pregnant, and the baby was due sometime around their first anniversary. He knew Bob would also want to be a father shortly after his wedding. Of course Randy was happy for all of them, but at the same time, watching Celeste's tummy grow was a stark reminder of what Randy knew he could never have. He could never get married, and he certainly couldn't ever be a father.

Carol clasped her hands, pressed them to her chest and spun around in a circle. "It's so wonderful to be in love. Haven't you ever been in love?" she asked melodramatically.

Randy's mouth opened, but no words came out. He couldn't say he ever had been in love. For too many years he'd been totally wrapped up in himself, doing only what he wanted, when he wanted, regardless of the cost to anyone else. Now he was paying the price, and he had to make sure that no one else had to pay the price with him, ever again.

He certainly didn't want some unfortunate woman to think he was marriage material. Now he had no one but God to answer to for his mistakes. It was better that way.

"I'm a free spirit," he said.

Carol sighed dramatically. "I know Lacey would be perfect for you."

"How can you say that? I've never even heard you mention her name before."

"I know. I've only met her a few times. She only started working next door last week."

"Last week?" Randy sputtered. "Then what makes you qualified to make such a statement?"

"A woman just knows these things."

"You don't know anything. Now quit fooling around. We'd better get back to work."

This time, Carol did leave him alone, but all day long, her words kept coming back to haunt him. He couldn't stop thinking about Lacey. She was kind of pretty, in a wholesome and unpretentious sort of way. She was also a few pounds heavier than what was considered fashionably thin, but that hinted at a lack of obsession with her weight. More important, it looked like she had strength of character, which was better than the superficial charm Carol displayed with skirts that were consistently too short to be respectable for someone doing retail sales.

Lacey, on the other hand, had been wearing a

modest, yet flattering outfit, even though working at a ladies' clothing store gave her the opportunity to select some pretty outrageous stuff.

In all things, including clothes, Carol vacillated between the ridiculous and the sublime. Yet, working with Carol was fun—their little play-fights often drove the rest of the staff nuts. It worked fine for him because a casual friendship was as far as he would go in a relationship.

Lacey seemed to be in a serious relationship. She was buying her significant other a computer, indicating that both her heart and her pocketbook were heavily involved.

As he was tidying up for the end of the day, he nearly dropped a pager on the floor when Lacey suddenly appeared in front of him, as if his thoughts had become reality.

"Hi. I was wondering if you had time to talk."

He unclipped his name badge and dropped it into his pocket. "It's actually the end of my shift, but I don't mind. In fact, the timing might even be good. If we go to the food court I can answer all your questions and we won't have to worry about other people interrupting."

"I heard that it's standing-room-only in the food court right now. But if you don't mind spending the time, we can go somewhere else to eat. I'll treat, since it's after working hours."

"I…" Randy let his voice trail off. It had been a long time since he'd been out to dinner with a woman, but he didn't feel right about having a woman pay.

He cleared his throat. "I have a better idea. I can write this off as a business expense, so let me pay. The only thing is that if we eat away from the mall, it will have to be walking distance."

"You want to walk? But…" She blinked a few times, then said, "That's fine, I don't mind."

Without warning, Carol joined them, grinning from ear to ear. She elbowed Randy in the ribs. "Are you two going somewhere?"

Randy stepped out of Carol's reach. "Yes. We're going out for dinner."

Carol glanced back and forth between Lacey and Randy, then turned directly to Lacey. "How are you getting there? Randy got his car towed away yesterday."

Randy gritted his teeth and turned to Lacey. "The parking lot control people towed it away. I'm sure you heard about the way they've decided to start enforcing the ban on staff parking in the public parking lot.

"The towing bill was really expensive. So I have to leave my car at home. How did you get here?"

Lacey's eyes widened. "Now I feel bad. When I took the job I was simply told it came with a parking spot. I didn't realize that parking was such a problem. It's okay. We can take my car. If you want, I can even give you a ride home."

He hesitated. "Wait a minute. If you got a parking spot, that means you're the store manager. I thought you were new."

"I was the assistant manager at the downtown store, but the manager here quit with no notice last week, so they offered me a transfer, as long as I started immediately. Things are a big mess, but this is a good promotion, so I couldn't turn it down."

Randy shrugged his shoulders. "Sorry. I didn't mean to sound bitter about the parking. I'm still trying to convince myself that it's for the best, because it's cheaper for my insurance. But it sure does make it inconvenient."

"Now I know why the rest of my staff take the bus."

"I don't take the bus. Ever. I used my inline skates to get here today. It was kind of fun, actually, but I may change my mind the next time it rains." Randy paused to check his watch. "We should get going. I just have to get my stuff from the back, and we can leave."

"…and then she told me her husband was a used car salesman!"

Randy nibbled on his lower lip, then allowed himself to laugh at his own joke, but only after Lacey laughed first.

Randy didn't know why he couldn't shut up. He

shouldn't have been nervous. It didn't matter if he couldn't remember the last time he'd taken a woman out for dinner. This wasn't a date. All he had to do was impress Lacey with his knowledge of computers, which was extensive. She didn't have to know anything else about him. He didn't even have to worry that she would want to—it was to his advantage that she already had someone.

He picked up his cup, wrapped his hands around it and rested his elbows on the table. "If I'd been thinking properly, I would have brought a catalog. In the store, all I do is point."

"It's okay. I know that you'll help me pick the best one. I just want to make sure it's a surprise."

Randy sighed. Not only had no one ever given him a surprise birthday party, no one had ever given him an expensive gift. Of course, he didn't expect such gifts from his friends. They routinely gave each other the standard guy-gifts—CD's, tools, computer paraphernalia and, lately, music books. The biggest surprise was when it was wrapped.

His family had never given gifts. Not that they couldn't afford them, they just never did. All his life he'd learned how to get by without asking or expecting anything. That way, he was never disappointed.

But lately, he'd seen the other side of the fence from his friends. Adrian had been thrilled at his latest birthday gift from Celeste, handmade mouse and keyboard covers that were cleverly made to look like a real mouse and a piece of cheese.

He focused back on Lacey. "Don't worry. I can hold the computer of your choice in the store until the day before the party. That way you don't have to worry about spoiling the surprise." He smiled and tried to turn on his "salesman patter." "You'll get a surprise, too, with how good a deal I'm going to give you on this computer. I'll even throw in a bunch of extras."

Lacey smiled back weakly. "I honestly don't know what's standard. I'm just going to have to trust you."

"Don't worry. I won't take advantage of you."

"Just remember that if I do find out one day that you charged me too much, I'm right next door, all day, every day."

Randy opened his mouth, but no words came out. He didn't know if she was teasing him, or if this really was some kind of warning. Either way, it intrigued him. The woman had guts, and he liked that.

He sipped his coffee, speaking over the rim of the cup. "You go right ahead and do all the comparison shopping you want. Then you'll know how good a deal I'm going to give you."

"That's fine. And the next time you come in to buy more panty hose, I'll do the same for you."

Randy choked on his coffee, then lowered the cup to the saucer. "Now just a minute. Those weren't for me, and I never..." His words trailed off when Lacey's stifled giggles broke through.

"Gotcha," she said from behind her coffee cup.

"Not funny," he pretended to grumble, struggling not to laugh back. He suddenly became very serious. "I need to know one more thing, and that's how much time you and...Bryce, was it? are going to spend together on it."

Lacey looked puzzle. "Together? None. I frankly don't see how some people spend hours and hours on the computer every day."

Randy smiled. "I couldn't be without my computer. Computers are my only source of income, so I have to keep up with all the latest and the greatest." He grinned wryly. "Sometimes my online activities make me late for practice on Wednesday nights, but, of course, I'm never late for work."

She stared blankly at him. Randy hadn't meant to get so personal, but his computer and all that went with it had played a big part in his recovery.

"What is it you're practicing? Are you in a league?" Lacey asked.

"Uh..." Randy felt his cheeks flush. "Actually, it's not sports, it's music, and it's my friends who are really practicing, not me. When we first started I tried to learn to play keyboards from a book, but that went about as well as you might expect, so they found someone else to do it. But Celeste is phenomenal.

Maybe even the best piano player I've ever met. So now I work the sound system and do all the computer stuff, which is right up my alley."

She smiled. "That sounds like fun. Does your band have a CD out?"

Randy laughed. "No. It's nothing like that. It's just the worship team for church."

"Just? Don't say that. The worship team is important. I think it's wonderful that you're utilizing your talents. I wish I could do something like that, but I don't seem to be good at anything besides sewing."

"That's a skill not everyone has. Maybe you can…" His voice trailed off. "Wait—you go to church?"

"Yes, I do."

Randy smiled. "Great! Would you like to join me in a short prayer before we eat? It's always awkward to ask that in work situations, or when you don't know someone very well."

"I was just thinking the same thing. I'd like that."

Just at that moment, the waiter arrived with their meals. Randy led with a short prayer, and they began to eat.

"So, did you move to Appleton recently?"

"No. I live downtown, where I just rent an apartment. Now that I have the new job, I think I'm going to move closer to it. Do you live near the mall?"

"Yes. I grew up not far away from here. It seemed natural to get a job in the neighborhood, too." More than that, his friend Bob knew Tom, the store owner. Because of Bob's reference, Tom offered Randy a job when no one else would consider him. He'd been there ever since, which was coming up on six years. And now he was the assistant manager.

"I'll never move. I live within two minutes of my friends, within five minutes of my church and ten minutes from my job." He didn't know why God blessed him like this, especially when he'd once blamed God for so much. But now his life was in order, and he didn't intend to ever change a thing.

Randy dunked one of his fries in the blob of ketchup, coating it just right. "Where do you go to church, then, if you live downtown?"

Lacey smiled, and her eyes turned dreamy as she spoke. "Every Sunday morning I drive back to the west end where I grew up and go with my family, and we spend the day together."

Randy nodded. He spent a lot of time at church, but it was with his friends. He couldn't remember the last time he'd seen his family. Usually it didn't bother him, but today, watching Lacey smile at her private thoughts, it reminded him of the big hole in his life. For the past few years he'd been so busy with his friends that he hadn't really noticed, but now that Adrian and Celeste were married and Bob was getting married, Randy had more time on his hands. Still, God always found things for him to do, and

Randy couldn't complain. "Lately I've been going to both the morning and evening services because I'm on the worship team, so that keeps me pretty busy on Sundays. It's sometimes a lot of work, but at the same time, it's also fun. And speaking of fun, I should tell you a little about the sidewalk sale that's coming up at work next week. Or rather, I should warn you."

Lacey's fork froze halfway to her mouth. "Warn me?"

"You can see some really funny things with bargain hunters. There's this one couple who always show up, and one of them always wears a disguise, as if we can't recognize him. I hear everyone's already making bets to see what he's going to do this year. Last year, the guy pretended to be a rich Texan— big hat, the drawl, everything. He even pasted on a fake mustache. You could tell it was fake because it was a different color than his hair, and it was crooked. It was hilarious." Randy grinned, remembering Carol's reaction when the man called her "L'il lady." He really thought Carol was going to kick him.

Randy sobered. "Seriously, though, you've got to watch out for them. He tries to distract the staff person at one end of the table while his partner, who is dressed normally, tries to steal something from the other end." He leaned forward over the table, and Lacey leaned forward in response.

"She always puts smaller items in her bra so no one will challenge her to put them back. But last year when I caught her and started calling the cops on my cell phone, she dug everything out real fast and ran."

Lacey gasped. "You're kidding!"

"I wish I was." Randy straightened. "But most of the time, the sidewalk sale is a lot of fun."

Lacey glanced from side to side. "Have you noticed that we're nearly the only ones here? I think we lost track of the time."

Randy looked around, confirming that she was indeed correct.

"Yeah. I guess we should go."

While he signaled the waiter for the bill, a strange sense of loss came over him. He couldn't remember the last time he'd enjoyed himself so much. He was at an age where most of the women he knew were sizing him up for a husband, so those situations quickly became awkward. God had shown him that he wasn't husband material, and he never would be.

But Lacey was marriage material. Randy couldn't help but think that her boyfriend was indeed one lucky man. Tonight, Randy had thoroughly enjoyed himself, but for tonight he was on borrowed time, and the lender had called in the loan. It was time to go home.

When she dropped him off in front of his apartment building, a surge of melancholy for what could never happen coursed through him.

Once inside, instead of settling down, Randy walked to the patio door to his balcony and looked out the window. They'd stayed at the restaurant so long that it was dark, and all the city lights were on. His suite faced downtown, so he had a good view from the seventeenth floor.

Randy stepped out onto the balcony to take in the city below. He couldn't make out specific details, but he could see the brightly colored lights of the mall in the distance.

He gazed over the expanse of the city, paying particular attention to the high-rise towers in the downtown core, wondering which building was Lacey's.

Chapter Two

"I'll be back in two hours, Kate," Lacey called as she stepped into the mall.

As she began walking toward the mall center, Lacey glanced into the computer store on her way past, but she didn't see Randy at work.

Randy.

Being out with him had almost felt like a date, except it wasn't. He was only helping her select the right computer for Bryce. Yet, after going out with him only once, she couldn't help but like him. In fact, he was almost too good to be real.

Lacey had learned the hard way that when something seemed too good to be true, it usually was.

She pushed thoughts of the charming salesman out of her head as she continued walking toward the mall's feature display of the week. The police department had set up a display to raise public awareness of the dangers of drinking and driving and Lacey had volunteered to help give out information at the booth.

Drunk driving had ruined her family and she didn't want to see it happen to anyone else.

Lacey didn't remember her father being a heavy drinker, but at the time, her perspective had been that of a child. Most of his drinking would have been at night, after she had been put to bed. Most of her memories of her father were good, doing typical family things together. Usually their family was happy, but she did remember her parents arguing after her father had been out with his friends. She remembered him acting rather strangely when he came home, but she hadn't known why. The only thing she knew then about her father's drinking was that he "went out for a drink" with his friends after work on paydays. On paydays, he always came home acting more strangely than other days.

It was on one payday that her father never came home again.

Because he died in an accident that he'd caused, and because he'd been drunk, no insurance would pay on the policy—not the auto insurance, nor the life insurance, and there was no life insurance on the mortgage. Slowly and painfully, over the next year, their home was foreclosed on, their savings were eroded and their extended family was torn apart. As she grew up, Lacey's most vivid memories were of her mother, crying, all alone, after she thought that Lacey and her brother and sister were sleeping.

Lacey didn't want the same thing to happen to anyone else, yet she saw it happening to Susan, her sister. No matter what Lacey said or did, she couldn't get Susan's husband, Eric, to see the risk he was creating for his family, and that if he died, the same thing would happen. Eric also wasn't taking into account the strangers who would be innocent victims if he continued on his path to self-destruction.

Eric insisted that he wasn't a serious drinker because he didn't drink every day. He often accused Lacey of trying to cause trouble between himself and Susan. Eric didn't know about the countless times Susan had called her in the middle of the night, worried because Eric still hadn't come home when she knew he was out drinking with his friends. On other days, Susan said she shouldn't have let the moment get to her, that Eric's drinking wasn't that bad.

Since those whom she loved wouldn't listen, the only thing Lacey could do was to try to help strangers.

As Lacey approached the display, a police officer was talking to the volunteer who would be working with her, as well as a woman who was packing up a few things, ready to leave.

Lacey's breath caught when she saw who she was to be her partner for the next hour.

"Randy. Hello."

The officer smiled at her. "I see you two already know each other. That's great. I'll leave Randy to show you what to do, and I'll get back to my area." He returned to the Breathalyzer and other equipment that was only for police use, leaving her alone with Randy.

Randy smiled as he wrote up a name tag for her. "We're supposed to split our time between pointing out different focus areas for people who try out and keeping the tables tidy, putting new brochures into the displays as people take them and just smiling and looking friendly."

Lacey nodded. "I can certainly do that. It's nice to see you volunteering your time."

"It's not really such a sacrifice. I have personal reasons for being here. A good friend was killed in a drinking-and-driving accident a few years back, and I want to do what I can to raise awareness. I know a lot of people, so maybe someone will recognize me and come and ask questions."

"Oh." Lacey's throat constricted. The only person killed in her father's accident had been her father, but she often lay awake at night, wondering if he'd ever caused an accident he either didn't know about, or wouldn't admit to, when someone swerved to avoid him. She didn't want to think that there could be, but she had to accept that it might have happened. It was too long ago to have been a connection between the death of her father and the death of Randy's friend, but that didn't mean it hadn't happened to someone else.

The possibility made her even more angry at how some people could be so irresponsible, both with their own lives, and of the lives of others around them.

She rested one finger on the schedule. "There are still a few slots not filled. I want to put my name down for another shift. What about you?"

He nodded. "I'm on the list for Saturday because that's the mall's busiest day."

"But you're off on Saturday, aren't you?"

"Yeah. That way I can be here for more than just the length of my lunch break."

Guilt raced through Lacey. She should have been giving up more of her time, too, but she had set Saturday aside to prepare for Bryce's party. Now, thinking that all she was doing was getting ready to do something fun, she felt selfish.

As she had been instructed, she began to tidy the piles of brochures, when a young couple entered the area. The woman approached her and asked for help to find a brochure that contained recipes for nonalcoholic punch. Lacey pointed to the Alternatives section and stepped aside.

While she waited, the young man approached Randy.

"Can you tell her that coffee is good enough, that she doesn't have to make something without alcohol for people?"

Randy's hands froze above the display he was re-arranging. "That's a very common myth, but it's not true. Coffee doesn't make a person sober up, neither does food. If you have something in your stomach you don't get drunk so fast, but you still get just as drunk. The only thing that sobers a person up is time."

The young man blinked. "That's not true. Coffee works."

Randy shook his head. "No. Coffee won't sober you up. It just makes you a wide-awake drunk. Caffeine is a stimulant. It's the stimulant that makes you think you're more sober than you actually are."

"That's not true, man. I know it works."

Lacey glanced toward the young woman to make sure she didn't need any more help, then stepped closer to the two men. She, too, had always believed that drinking coffee would help a person to sober up. She'd been with Susan often, helping to make coffee so it would be ready for when Eric got home after an evening of being out with his friends.

The only thing wrong with that scenario was that Eric had already driven home by the time he started drinking the coffee.

Randy pulled out one of the brochures and handed it to the young man. "Sorry, but the only thing about coffee that sobers you up is the time it takes to drink it. Water does the same, except it doesn't make you need to go to the bathroom as much, and it doesn't leave you hyper."

The young man slapped the brochure onto the table without opening it. "I don't need this propaganda."

Randy picked up a pen, scribbled something on the brochure, then handed it back. "Then check out this coffee manufacturer's Web site or check out a few search engines. Everything will tell you the same thing. If your guests drink, have a designated driver, or be a responsible host and budget money for cab fare. In some states, the host may be held legally responsible if their guests drive home drunk and have an accident."

The young man froze. "What?"

Randy crossed his arms over his chest. "Think about it."

The young man stepped back, and stomped to the lady he'd arrived with. She quickly picked out one of every brochure in the row, and the two of them hurried away.

Lacey stared at Randy. "How do you know all that stuff?"

"I just do."

She waited for him to say more, but he didn't.

"Randy, I was wondering—"

Behind her, a middle-aged man entered the display area, cutting off her question.

"Excuse me. I was wondering if you could tell me some information about roadside suspensions."

Randy pointed to the police officer who was on the other side of the display area. "He's the man to ask about legal matters."

The man backed up a step. "No way. I'm not asking the police. I'm only asking about it for a friend."

From the looks of the man's bloodshot eyes, Lacey found that highly unlikely.

"I really can't comment," Randy said, "but if you want to know at what point blood alcohol levels result in a roadside suspension, you can read these brochures."

Randy picked brochures off a number of piles, gathered them together, then offered the man one specifically on suspensions.

Lacey's throat tightened. Roadside suspensions were much more common today than when she was a child. If her father's license had been suspended, he might still be alive, and her life would have been very different.

The man reached out and accepted all of the pamphlets.

Randy stepped back and tapped a picture of a man in a jail cell, presumably the drunk tank. "But before you think of the legal ramifications, you should think about what it would be like to be without your car.

After court, a twenty-four-hour suspension could go further, resulting in a driving prohibition, plus a fine, depending on the severity of the offence and prior records. If that happened, how would you get to work? What would you say to people who asked why you always needed a ride wherever you went? You'd have to worry about increased insurance premiums once you get your license back, on top of all that. Ask yourself if it's worth it to have a few drinks before getting into the car."

The man's face paled and he dropped all the brochures but one. "I'll tell my friend that," he muttered, turned and walked away.

"Wow," Lacey exclaimed. "You're good here. No wonder you're doing this. You know so much."

"Yeah," Randy said quickly, then spun around and began to straighten out the brochures the man with the bloodshot eyes had dropped.

Lacey stepped closer. "All I was going to do was smile and hand out brochures. You're really getting up close and personal. You're having quite an effect on people."

"It's a gift," Randy mumbled, not looking up at her.

She stared at him as he continued to tidy up piles she thought were quite straight enough.

She knew Randy was very inconvenienced being unable to take his car to work due to the increased parking security, and it impressed her that he was using that knowledge and experience in a constructive way.

Unless he knew so much about having a driver's license suspended from more personal experience....

Lacey shook her head at the wayward direction of her thoughts. The concept that Randy could ever have had his license suspended because of drinking was preposterous. They had been out together for supper at a restaurant where alcoholic drinks were readily available, and the issue hadn't even come up. Randy was also a committed Christian, active in his church. The only reason he didn't have his car was because of the new parking regulations.

Which reminded her that Randy currently needed transportation.

Lacey spoke quickly, before someone else came to browse at the display. "Would you like a ride home again tonight?"

He smiled hesitantly.

Lacey's foolish heart fluttered.

"Yeah, I'd like that. Thanks."

"Maybe we can do dinner again and talk more about Bryce's computer? I don't want to wait until the last minute and run out of time."

"Sure. We can do that."

"Then I'll see you at five."

The new volunteer arrived at the booth, right on time, ending their conversation. Randy waved to the police officer at the other end to signal his pending departure, and turned back to Lacey.

"See you later," he said, and walked away.

Adrian Braithwaite unplugged the cord from between his guitar and the amp, wound it, fastened the Velcro strap and tossed it into the bin.

"You were late today," he said as he watched Randy unplug another cord and do the same. "I thought you were going to be early. I even bought extra doughnuts."

"I can't take my car to work anymore."

"That didn't really answer my question."

"You didn't ask a question."

Adrian waited for Randy to say more, but Randy didn't elaborate. Not only did he not elaborate, Randy didn't come up with a hundred and one far-fetched excuses, nor did he respond with a lame joke. He was also very busy cleaning up instead of hiding in the kitchen eating the extra half a box of doughnuts while everyone else put everything away.

Something wasn't right. And Adrian was going to find out what it was.

"Then how did you get to work?"

"I've been using my inline skates."

Adrian frowned. "Really? Why didn't you just take the bus? Oh, wait." Adrian paused, remembering incidents from their younger days when he, Bob,

Randy and their other friend Paul had taken the bus on many of their excursions. He couldn't count the times they all had to disembark in a hurry because Randy had to go throw up, even when they sat in the front while they traveled to their chosen destination of the day. Randy's parents laughed it off, but Bob's mother always came to give them a ride whenever Randy couldn't get back on the bus after being so violently sick.

"You don't still get motion sickness, do you? I can see using the skates to get to the mall, but it's quite an uphill journey back. How do you get home? Do you walk?" Walking home from work would explain why Randy was late, but not why Randy was being so evasive about it. He looked out the window to Randy's car parked on the street. "You've got your car now."

"I got a ride home, and I took my own car from there."

"Now we're getting somewhere. But if you got a ride, how in the world could you have been late?"

Randy's movements quickened as he turned the levels on the sound board down to zero, and began unplugging the unit. "Because we went out for dinner before she took me home," Randy told him, barely audible.

Adrian nearly dropped the microphone in his hand. "She? You mean, like a woman?"

Randy tossed another neatly wrapped cord into the bin with far more force than was necessary. "No. A dog drove me home. What do you think?"

"You don't have to get so sarcastic. I was only asking." He moved in closer to Randy. "What's she like?"

Randy dragged one hand down his face. "She's different than any woman I've ever met before. Funny, but not by telling jokes…she's witty. Smart. Unbelievably organized. Modest, if people use words like that anymore. I haven't known her for more than a few days, but I feel good being with her. I know it's wrong, but I can't help it. I keep thinking about her. I don't know what it is. For the past couple of days, we've started out talking about computers, but then we end up talking about something else, and we have a lot of fun. So much fun that it will almost be worth it when her boyfriend shows up and punches my lights out."

Adrian blinked. "Boyfriend? If she's got a boyfriend, what are you doing going out with her?"

Using his toes, Randy pushed at a guitar pick lying on the carpet. "I'm not really going out with her. She's buying him a computer for his birthday, and she has a lot of questions, so we've been going out for dinner, just to talk. I also don't want to look a gift horse in the mouth when she offers me a ride, because then I don't have to kill myself skating home."

"If she's got a boyfriend, regardless of the reason you're getting together, it must be pretty awkward."

Randy turned toward Adrian. "You want to hear awkward? She's invited me to his birthday party."

"Are you going?"

"Yeah. She asked me to put the computer together for him. It's a surprise."

Adrian winced. "And you're okay with that?"

"No, but I don't have any choice. She said she'll give me a ride home every day this week, and I have to return the favor."

Memories flooded Adrian of his initial contacts with his wife, Celeste. In hindsight, he could now see how much she'd affected him, and it had all happened so quickly. Adrian wanted to caution Randy about the same thing, because he knew how Randy felt about relationships, especially with his background. But before he could figure out how to put the words together, Randy stood up.

"Adrian, I feel really tired all of a sudden. I think whatever is happening with this woman is getting to me, and I can't let that happen. I'm going to go home and read my Bible for a little while, and then I should see if anyone from my chat group is online. I need to talk to someone."

Before Adrian had a chance to volunteer to talk to Randy in person instead of having Randy go to his online support group, Randy turned around and left.

Without first stopping in the kitchen and raiding the doughnuts.

"Uh-oh…" Adrian said as he heard Randy's car squeal off in the distance.

"I can't talk now, Mom. I'm at work. But I have a price for the computer."

Lacey nodded at another customer who entered the store, made a few quick calculations, then whispered the figures to her mother.

"Will you be going out with that young man after work again?"

Lacey's fingers froze over the calculator. "Probably."

"How well do you know him? I mean, *really* know him?"

"Uh…not a lot…."

"You've already bought the computer so you don't need to see him again. Just be careful."

Lacey gulped. She knew what her mother meant. Her family had a history of making bad choices when it came to men, from her father to her brother-in-law. Lacey was very likely to follow her mother's and her sister's patterns—it was obviously in her genes. And that was why Lacey had decided that she would never get married.

"I will." Lacey hung up the phone, but instead of returning to her work, her hand stayed on the phone as she stared at the wall. The wall between her store and the computer store. Randy was on the other side of that wall.

She knew she didn't have to see him again, but she would anyway. She really hadn't needed to invite him to Bryce's party to set up the computer, either.

The only reason she was continuing to see him was because he needed a ride.

If there was anything she'd learned from all her hardships growing up, it was the pain of what it was like to do without. When she started going to church and the people there discovered the financial plight of her family, many stepped in to help. Their outpouring of kindness, help and financial assistance was the first thing that opened her heart, as well as the hearts of her family, to God's love. At times it was humiliating to take charity. But it was also a lesson in how to accept graciously, as well as how to give sacrificially.

That was why she wanted to give Randy a ride home every day. Simply because he needed it. There was no other reason. Really.

She jerked her hand away from the phone and continued with her task of checking inventory for the sidewalk sale, but she was soon interrupted by a customer.

The woman closed her eyes briefly and inhaled deeply as she slid a pair of earrings toward the cash register. "It's really hot out there. It must be so nice to work in here, where it's air-conditioned."

Lacey sighed. "Maybe, but I'm missing out on one

of the last really hot days of the summer. It's different when you don't have a choice."

The woman shrugged her shoulders. "Suit yourself."

After the woman left, the comment about the hot weather outside stuck on Lacey like a burr. When the rush died down, she retrieved her lunch from the fridge and called out to Kate, "I'm going to take my break outside. I'll see you in half an hour."

Lacey smiled at the blast of heat as she stepped outside and headed straight for the small park next door. A gazebo sheltered people from the hot sun, and beside the gazebo, a patch of trees provided shade, where a number of people were sitting or lying on blankets. Blankets weren't her thing, but half an hour of sunshine sure was.

On the other side of the park a few benches lined the sidewalk, which was beside a small bed of flowers. Unlike the gazebo and the area under the trees, the benches were vacant because they were in the full sun.

Lacey headed for the benches.

Everything was fairly quiet, until the sound of a soft, clattery rumble began. She turned her head to see a lone man on inline skates approaching from the other side of the park.

She recognized the man, even from the distance.

Since he was coming quite fast, Lacey moved to the side of the path so he could pass without difficulty.

"Hi, Randy," she said as he whizzed past.

The noise of the skates on the cement sidewalk stopped instantly. Lacy spun around, expecting to see Randy lying on the ground. Her heart pounded as she watched him, running on the grass, slowing his speed until he came to a stop. He turned around, stepped back onto the sidewalk and skated back to her.

"Lacey? What are you doing out here?" He switched the box he was carrying to his other hand and checked his watch.

She held up her lunch bag. "I'm taking a late break. What are you doing out here at this hour?"

He held out the box and grinned. "I missed my doughnuts last night, so I went to the doughnut shop on my coffee break."

"You couldn't get a doughnut in the mall?"

He shook his head. "These are special. You can't get these in the mall." He opened the box, displaying a half-dozen specialty Boston Cremes. "Want one? They're my favorite."

She reached forward, then froze before she actually touched one. "I shouldn't. I haven't had my lunch yet."

"It's okay. I promise not to tell your mother that you had your dessert before the main course."

Lacey's stomach churned. She still wasn't sure that she wanted to introduce him to her mother, but by inviting him to Bryce's party, she'd opened herself up to her mother's justifiable curiosity.

Grinning, Randy held the box out, and winked. Lacey's fingers trembled as she reached into the box. "Speaking of my mother and the party, I still haven't figured out how to get you into the house early enough to set everything up before everyone else gets there."

"I don't know, either," Randy mumbled as he bit into one of the doughnuts. "All I do know is that I won't be available until after eleven-thirty, because that's when my church's service ends."

"Really? My church ends the service at noon." Lacey's mind raced and she stiffened, steeling her courage in order to ask her question. "How about if I go to church with you? Then we could be back at Mom's house half an hour earlier than everyone else. Would that be enough time to set up the computer for Bryce? That's about the amount of time I'll need to do the food."

"Yeah. It would," Randy said around the doughnut sticking out his mouth, keeping it clenched between his teeth as he closed the lid of the box and tried to press the tape back down. Unable to make the tape stick, he grasped the doughnut again and took it out of his mouth so he could speak. "I've been thinking. What is Bryce going to say when he sees me with you at his birthday party? Do you think he'll be okay with that?"

Lacey nodded and hurried to swallow her bite of

the pastry. "Of course he'll be fine with it. In fact, I'm almost sure that the two of you will spend quite a bit of time together with the computer, after all the excitement dies down a bit."

Randy's eyes widened, and he continued to pick at the tape. "Oh," he muttered.

Lacey waited for him to say more, but he remained silent.

"If you're worried that you won't know anyone there, it's okay. Everyone is all friends and family. Besides, I'm sure once Bryce discovers what you do for a living, he'll hog you to himself all day. Please don't be shy."

For an almost indiscernible second, Randy stiffened. Lacey almost wanted to smile, except she was still too nervous. Despite her words, even though she hadn't known him that long, she suspected the last thing anyone could ever accuse Randy of was being shy.

"I guess," he mumbled. "I really should go. It was faster going on the skates than walking, but I think I've used up my fifteen minutes, and I don't want to be late getting back to work. I guess I'll see you Sunday."

"Sure. What time should I pick you up?"

Randy had begun to push off, but he stopped and spun around. "If you're going to my church, then I think good manners dictate that I should pick you up. After all, you're going to be my guest. It's just that I have to be there an hour early in order to set up the sound system for the worship team."

"That's fine. I don't mind. Would you like a ride home again tonight? You're pretty good on those skates, but it is a long way uphill. I can give my address and directions after work. Maybe over dinner?"

"I…" Randy's voice trailed off, and eventually, he nodded. "Sure. That would be great."

"Good. I'll see you at five o'clock." Because he'd sounded hesitant, Lacey turned and started walking toward the bench, not waiting for his reply.

She didn't want to admit it to herself, but she wouldn't have been able to bear it if he had said no.

Chapter Three

"What does this button do?"

"Uh…Lacey… Please don't touch that."

Lacey yanked her hand away.

"Thanks," Randy muttered as he held one of the earpieces of the headphones up to his ear with one hand, and adjusted another setting with the other.

While Randy adjusted knobs and buttons, Lacey watched his friends on the worship team practice. They were easy to see from the height of the sound booth, which was in a raised room at back of the sanctuary, recessed into the back wall.

"Okay, I've got everything set." Randy put the headphones down on the table beside the very complex-looking soundboard, and gave the worship team a thumbs-up signal. "Now we sit back and wait for the service to begin. I'll have to make a few adjustments as the room fills up, but this is pretty much it."

"I've never thought about what happens behind the scenes on Sunday mornings. This is actually quite interesting."

"The same things happen at every church, every Sunday, including yours. Speaking of your church, you think anyone will miss you?"

Lacey shrugged her shoulders. "No, and Mom thinks it's perfect. When Bryce and mom left this morning, the house would have looked normal. Since we'll be able to get back so much earlier we can let everyone in to hide without anyone having to rush. When Mom and Bryce finally get back, Bryce will really be surprised."

Randy stiffened and blinked. "Bryce lives with your mother?"

Lacey turned to him. "For now, but he's going to move into the dormitory for his last year of university. Mom's already started complaining about how much he eats, and saying how good it will be that he's moving out, but we both know that she'll be lonely without him. Of course he'll move back home when he's done with classes, but who knows for how long? I don't think it will take him long to get a job. He'll probably work for a while to pay off his student loans, and then move out when he's financially stable. Maybe he'll even get married. Mom says he's been getting a lot of calls from a woman lately."

She expected Randy to make some kind of comment, but he was strangely silent. His eyes visibly widened, and he stared at her.

She couldn't figure out what he thought was strange about her story, although she couldn't really remember talking to him previously about her mother, or about Bryce. Of all the things they'd talked about, family was something that had never entered a conversation, hers or his. She'd even had the impression that he avoided the topic. Thinking about it now made her suddenly curious.

"I guess I didn't tell you. My dad died when we were kids. My sister is older than me, and she's been married for a while. I moved out when I got the job downtown. So now it's just Bryce and Mom left at the house."

"I'm so sorry. Not about your brother. About your dad. That must have been awful."

Lacey swallowed hard. She'd almost told him about it at the booth in the mall, but she couldn't bring herself to talk about it then. With the church service about to start soon, she didn't want to talk about it now, either. Yet she knew she had to tell him something, so he wouldn't accidentally upset her mother by saying the wrong thing, not knowing what had happened.

She lowered her gaze to the floor. "When he died, he left Mom with three small kids. We had a lot of struggles but we made it, with a lot of help. After Bryce finished high school he worked for a couple of years, then managed to get a student loan for university. He's been living at home, but Mom sees how hard the commute is, so she told him that for this last year, he should stay in the dorm. It's going to be best for Bryce, but hard on my mom. When Bryce moves out next week, Mom's going to be all alone for the first time. She's devoted her life to us kids."

Randy cleared his throat. "So you must be older than, uh, your brother?"

"Yes. I'm three years older than Bryce, and two years younger than Susan. Are you okay? Your voice sounds funny. Are you coming down with a cold?"

He cleared his throat again and touched his fingertips to his neck. "No. I think I just have a frog in my throat. I'm fine."

Lacey tipped her head to the side. "I probably should have said something sooner, but we never seem to talk about family."

His whole body stiffened. "I don't have much to tell. I didn't live with my parents all the time. I sometimes lived at my best friend's parents' house." He turned and began to play with some of the settings on the soundboard.

She waited for him to continue, but he didn't.

Despite his claim that there wasn't much to tell, Lacey suspected there was. She turned toward the sanctuary, which was starting to fill up. "Are any of them here? Can I meet them?"

"Unfortunately, my parents don't go to church, and Bob's parents don't go here. They go to the church across from the arena, where I used to go, as well. The associate pastor from there, along with Bob, Adrian, Paul and I, and a small group of other people, started this church. We've come a long way from twenty-seven people, don't you think?"

"Wow. I'm impressed."

"It's God's work, not mine, or anyone else's in the ministry team."

The worship team stopped playing and left the stage and Randy switched to a CD, setting it to play softly in the background.

"Are you going to join your friends? I mean, at my church, the worship team always prays before the service."

"Usually I would, but I don't want to leave you here all alone."

"It's okay. I'll be fine. Go pray with your friends."

He turned to go, paused and then left.

While Randy was gone, Lacey watched as the sanctuary continued to fill up.

Even though it was her first time here, she felt

comfortable. But that shouldn't have been a surprise. It appeared that Randy hadn't had a happy childhood, yet he had settled into a niche that was good for him. He'd found good friends, a good church, and he was happy.

Lacey smiled. Randy was more than just happy; she thoroughly enjoyed his offbeat sense of humor.

The past few days she found that she could hardly wait for the end of the day so she could see Randy again.

Her smile dropped. After the party was over, she wouldn't have any reason to see Randy. Unless, of course, she continued to give him a ride home every day.

Lacey's heart began to pound.

If she had been trying to tell herself that she wasn't attracted to Randy, she was only deluding herself. She did like him, and she was starting to like him a lot. But she needed to find out more about him, including how he felt about her.

"I'm back. Did you miss me?"

She had missed him, but she didn't want to admit it, so she merely shrugged her shoulders.

He grinned. "Good. I missed you, too."

Lacey quickly sent up a prayer of thanks to God for the answer to one of the questions she hadn't yet dared to ask.

Randy flipped a switch, and a screen floated

down. He flipped another switch and hit a few buttons on a computer beside the soundboard, and the words to the first worship song appeared.

Lacey focused her attention on the screen, and pushed all other thoughts out of her mind.

This was not the time to think about what might happen between herself and Randy. She was at church and she was there to set some time aside to worship God, not think about her personal life.

But after the party maybe, just maybe, she would have her answers.

"Surprise!"

Lacey watched Bryce's face pale, then turn ten shades of red. All their friends and family laughed, then broke out into applause. Beside him, their mother squealed with delight.

"We did it," Lacey whispered to Randy. "Look at him! He's really surprised."

"I think he's past surprised. He's gone into shock."

Lacey ran forward and gave her brother a big hug, which made everyone in the room cheer and applaud even more.

"I don't know what to say," Bryce admitted as he glanced back and forth at the room full of people.

Following her example, their niece and nephew, Kaitlyn and Shawn, also ran forward. Kaitlyn leaped into Bryce's arms.

"Happy birthday, Uncle Bryce!" Kaitlyn squealed with glee. "We all gots you a surprise!"

Bryce smiled and gave Kaitlyn a hug. "Yes, I'm sure surprised," he said, giving her a peck on the cheek.

Lacey removed Kaitlyn from Bryce's arms and set her on the floor. "Go see your mom, okay, Kaitlyn?" she whispered, then took Bryce by the hand and pulled him in the direction of his bedroom.

"What are you doing?" His voice lowered. "Everyone is following us. I didn't make my bed this morning."

Lacey barely suppressed a giggle. "Don't worry. The next surprise is that I made your bed for you. Just don't expect it to ever happen again."

That said, she shuffled behind him, and gave him a gentle nudge into the room, where Randy had set up the new computer on Bryce's desk. On the monitor, the multicolored message "Happy Birthday!" rolled across the screen.

Bryce's mouth dropped open. "What have you done?"

"Happy birthday!" everyone chorused behind him.

As Bryce disappeared from her side to go to the desk, Randy shuffled in to take Bryce's place beside her.

Bryce picked up the large card, which Randy had set on top of the keyboard, and opened it. While

Bryce read the card and responded to everyone as he read their comments, more people continued to squeeze into the small bedroom to watch.

The more the room filled up, the closer she and Randy had to move together, until he was pressed into her from her shoulder to her knee.

She looked up to his face to see if she could judge his response. Almost as if he could sense her movement, he turned his head and looked down at her.

His voice lowered to a husky whisper. "Hi," he muttered, and at the same moment as he spoke, his fingers intertwined with hers, and he gave her hand a gentle squeeze.

Lacey blushed. She didn't know what to do, and she didn't know if they should be holding hands, but she didn't want to let go. She also had to accept his action as a signal that something was happening between them, and that he felt the same way she did.

The room quieted as Bryce lowered the card. "Thank you, everyone. I don't know what to say."

Everyone started talking at the same time, offering their suggestions, mostly about taking turns using the new computer.

Lacey raised herself on her tiptoes and leaned toward Randy so he could hear her. "Do you want to show him how to work everything?"

He leaned back down to reply. "It's just a standard computer. He'll know what to do. I'll help him set up his e-mail and configure the settings later, when he's not the center of attention."

"I don't know. He looks a little flustered."

Bryce chose that moment to look directly at Lacey. His lost expression made up her mind. She tightened her grip on Randy's hand and led him a few steps forward, until they were standing beside the chair where Bryce sat.

"Bryce, this is Randy. He's the one who helped me buy the computer."

Bryce stood. As he caught a glimpse of their joined hands, he raised his eyebrows. He looked up and shook Randy's free hand. "That must have been a challenge. Lacey is afraid of computers."

"Am not," Lacey retorted.

Bryce looked at her, but spoke to Randy. "She is."

Randy grinned. "But she's learning."

Lacey released Randy's hand and stepped back. "I should go help in the kitchen. Everyone is probably starving." She pressed through the crowd and hurried to the kitchen, where her mother and her sister were busily removing the canapés from the oven and setting them on serving platters.

"Mom. Susan. It looks like we're almost ready. Things are going really well."

Her mother stopped fussing with the food, and straightened. "He was so surprised! And there are so many more people here than I expected. This is wonderful. But this means there are more people to feed."

That so many had been invited was no surprise to Lacey. The rented home was small, the furnishings were worn, but everyone was always welcome, and her mother had a habit of being generous when inviting people for a celebration that involved food. There had been many times in their family's history when God had provided for them when they couldn't provide for themselves. Now that their family was doing better, her mother did her best to provide for others, despite her humble means.

Lacey swept one hand through the air, above the table, which was covered with trays of food. "You still have enough for double the amount of people here. I don't know why you do this."

Her mother grinned, and reached into the oven for the second tray. "I can't let anyone go home hungry."

Lacey turned to Susan, who was pressing the candles into the cake. "I was thinking about putting the cake in the middle of the dining room table, but I don't know if there will be enough room."

Susan spoke without raising her head. "I've already moved the centerpiece. It's fine."

Lacey froze. Susan's voice had been too quiet, and too controlled. Added to the fact that Susan hadn't looked at her when she spoke, it gave Lacey a bad feeling in the pit of her stomach that had nothing to do with hunger.

"Susan, what's wrong?"

"Nothing," Susan answered quietly without looking up, which was all the answer Lacey needed. Something was definitely wrong, and it could only be something to do with Eric.

Lacey struggled to remember if she'd seen Eric in the crowd. She hadn't.

Lacey helped carry the food into the dining room. Her mother called everyone to eat, and after one of the men from her church paused for a prayer of thanks, the guests descended on the food like a swarm of locusts.

Out of the corner of her eye, Lacey noticed that Bryce and Randy filled their plates quickly and quietly, then disappeared back into the bedroom together.

Since they were obviously occupied, Lacey returned to the kitchen, where she found Susan, sitting at the table with her head bowed, picking more than she was eating.

Lacey sat beside Susan, speaking quietly and softly. "What's wrong?"

Susan pushed at a mushroom cap with her fork. "Same ol', same ol'," she grumbled.

What was wrong didn't take much imagination. Eric had obviously been drinking again, and done something to hurt Susan. The only unknown was that

Lacey didn't know if this time he'd spent too much money, dipping into the mortgage money to buy drinks for his friends at the bar, if he'd damaged the car, if he'd done something to hurt Susan's feelings or all of the above. Since it was the weekend, it wasn't likely that he'd lost another job because of his uncontrollable drinking habits. Unless he'd been out with his supervisor and started a fight with him.

Lacey didn't want to ask, so she remained silent. She only wanted to be there for Susan, regardless of what Eric had done.

Susan started to sniffle, but she didn't raise her head. "Do you remember Grampa's old violin?"

"Yes. Especially when he used to put on that old hat and play those funny songs, just to amuse us. But I also remember times he played those sad, haunting melodies. I've never heard anyone play a violin like Grampa."

Susan sniffled again. "You know that I've got his violin, right?"

Lacey nodded, her stomach dropping.

"I had it in the china cabinet, so when the kids are old enough to appreciate it, maybe they might take lessons."

"That's a sweet idea."

A big, fat tear rolled down Susan's cheek. "I don't know why he did it, but Eric took the violin out of the cabinet this afternoon. I knew he'd been drinking, so I told him to put it back. He just laughed and started fooling around with it, pretending he was playing it. But it slipped out of his hands, bounced off the coffee table and then he accidentally stepped on it." More tears flowed down Susan's cheeks; a few dripped onto her plate of untouched food.

Lacey's gut clenched. "Can it be fixed?"

"I don't know. Even if it can, we don't have that kind of money right now. Then, when Eric saw how upset I was, he got mad at me. He said I was trying to make him feel guilty. I told him it wasn't his fault." Susan sniffled again. "But he didn't calm down. We had a big fight in front of the children, and I said a few things that I now regret. That's something I told myself would never happen."

Lacey held back telling Susan that regrets or not, whatever she had said was probably right. Lacey also wanted to tell Susan that Eric was never going to change, but that wasn't quite true. Eric *had* changed in the past ten years. Every year he became steadily worse.

"I don't know what to say."

"I can't take it anymore. I think I'm going to go to counseling."

Lacey leaned across the table and rested her hand on Susan's arm. "That's good, but you're not the one who needs counseling. It's Eric."

"He won't go. He says he doesn't have a problem. He says he can quit anytime he wants."

Lacey bit her tongue. She couldn't count the number of times Eric had quit drinking, but it was exactly the same number of times he'd fallen off the wagon. And every time it was Susan who landed with a thud. His drinking was ruining Susan's life and their marriage. It wasn't good for their two children, either.

A couple of verses from Proverbs 23 that her mother had quoted when Susan had said she was going to marry Eric once again echoed through Lacey's head.

> Do not gaze at wine when it is red,
> when it sparkles in the cup,
> when it goes down smoothly!
> In the end it bites like a snake
> and poisons like a viper.

Indeed, Eric had poisoned his life, and he was poisoning the lives of his family. He didn't seem to care what his drinking did to anyone; he only continued to drink himself deeper into a hole.

Most days, Lacey tried her best to pray for him, and every day, she tried not to hate him.

She opened her mouth to tell Susan that she had to do something more than just counseling for herself, that no magic solution was going to fall from the sky, but before she could speak the sound of footsteps clicked on the tile floor behind her.

Bryce's voice broke the silence. "Lacey, have you seen my MP3 player? Oh. Hi, Susan. Thanks for contributing to the computer. It sure was a surprise."

Lacey quickly spun around in the chair to see that Bryce wasn't alone; Randy was beside him. She looked at both men and tried to signal Bryce with her eyes to leave the room. Bryce took the hint and walked out as if nothing was happening, but instead of leaving, Randy moved closer and leaned toward Lacey's face.

"Have you got something in your eye? If you want I can—" Randy's words came to a sudden stop when his attention wandered to Susan, who did have something in her eye. Both eyes. Tears. Which were streaming down her face.

He straightened, and his whole body went stiff. "Is something wrong? Do you need help?"

Susan swiped her arm over her eyes, which only smeared her makeup, making her look worse. "I'm sorry. There's nothing you can do. There's nothing anyone can do. It's my husband. I should go. I'm sorry you had to see me like this."

Susan stood, but Lacey blocked her path. "Where are you going to go? Is he home? Is he…" She let her words hang. There were times Lacey feared that as the situation continued to escalate, the day might come that Eric might hit Susan. She prayed daily that things would never get to that.

Susan must have thought the same thing at the same time, because she sank back down into the chair and covered her face with her hands. "You're right. He's probably in worse condition than when I left, and I know I'm being a bad wife, but I can't deal with that right now."

Randy stepped closer to Susan. "What's wrong? Is he sick? Is there anything anyone can do?"

She shook her head without taking her hands from her face. "No. It's not like that. He's not sick. He's... he's..." Her voice shook and trailed off as she raised her tear-streaked face. Lacey moved closer to Randy to tell Susan without words that he was with her, and that it was okay to keep talking. Once Susan figured that out, she looked straight at Randy. "My husband is at home, drunk. He was so bad I told him to stay home, not to come to my own brother's birthday party. That's so wrong. I don't know what to do anymore."

Lacey didn't know what to say, but somehow having Randy beside her made her feel stronger, and not as helpless as she always did whenever Susan's husband went off the deep end.

Randy's voice dropped to a soothing murmur. "I'm sorry. It sounds like he's got a serious drinking problem."

"I used to say that he didn't, that he could stop anytime, but I think I was just fooling myself. Yes, he has stopped, but he never stops for long, and every time he starts again it's worse than the time before." The tears started flowing again down Susan's cheeks, and her lower lip trembled. "I wish I knew how to make it stop."

Lacey slipped her hand into his, once again intertwining their fingers. She needed his strength now, more than anything. Susan finally admitting the magnitude of Eric's problem was good. She was glad Randy was with her. Maybe God did sometimes drop people out of the sky because, as always, Randy was a good listener, and Susan was definitely talking.

"Did Pastor Luke talk to him?" Lacey asked.

Susan lowered her hands, and looked up at Lacey with the most woeful expression she'd ever seen. "Yes. Pastor Luke warned Eric that he was going to destroy his family and our marriage. All it did was make Eric drink even more."

Randy didn't release Lacey's hand, but kept it firmly encased in his own as he lowered himself to rest on one knee so he could speak to Susan at eye level while she sat hunched over in the kitchen chair.

"If you don't mind me saying, he can't stop drinking if he's going to do it for you. I know that sounds harsh, but it's the truth. The only way he's going to quit drinking is if he quits for himself. It's not even a question of motivation. I'm sure you're giving him plenty of motivation. I hate to say this, but you might be making it easy for him to keep drinking by not making him take the consequences for his actions, and excusing him. Even if he's trying, it's like giving him permission to fail, which is different than accepting failure. It can be a steady downward spiral, and there's only one way out. That's to get help from God and other people who have the same problem and want to overcome it bad enough. He can do it, but he can't do it alone."

Lacey closed her mouth, wondering how long she'd been standing there with it hanging open. While Randy did have some serious moments, she'd never known him to be so profound.

She looked down at him, remembering the insight he'd shared with people at the drinking and driving public service booth in the mall.

A million thoughts flashed through Lacey's mind. Even though he wouldn't tell her what had happened, she knew that something unhappy lurked in his past.

All of her own past unhappiness had been a direct result of alcohol abuse. She'd dearly loved her father, and as a child listening to her parents argue about his drinking had been a horrible. Years later her mother still hadn't recovered fully, and now her sister was so miserable from the effects of alcohol abuse in her own marriage that she was crying and pouring out her heart to someone she didn't know.

Bryce had different struggles. Their father had been tough on Bryce because he was a boy. Being the youngest, Bryce had been the most helpless when their family troubles were at their worst. But because he had been so young when their father died, Bryce didn't have the same vivid memories, or nightmares, as the rest of them.

Randy knew so much, but there had to be a reason he wouldn't talk about his past. She didn't want to think that he'd suffered, too. She liked him too much for that.

"How do you know so much about all this stuff?" she choked out.

He turned his head up to face her, but remained kneeling in front of Susan.

"I know because I've been there. I'm an alcoholic, too."

Chapter Four

Randy didn't think it was a good sign when the second the words were out of his mouth, Lacey went rigid. He wanted to tell her not to worry, but his words caught in his throat as all the color drained from her face.

Before he could move, Lacey yanked her hand out of his and stepped back.

Randy scrambled to his feet. "It's not what you think. I haven't had a drink for six years. I'm fine."

"Eric says he's fine all the time. He's far from fine."

"That's different."

"You can't say that. You've never met Eric."

"No, but I've met lots of people like him. Maybe I could even have been like him at one time. But I have God in my life, and everything is different now." He pressed his palm over his heart. "With God's continuing grace, I'll never have another drink until the day I die."

Her wide eyes and pale complexion told him she didn't believe him.

"Lacey…please… I'm telling the truth."

She stared at him, her eyes still wide. "I know you're thirty-one now. How old were you when you became an alcoholic?"

His gut clenched so bad, he felt like he might throw up. "I started drinking heavily when I was fifteen, but I don't know exactly when I crossed the line that I could have been labeled as an alcoholic. The important thing is that I quit the day after my twenty-fifth birthday, and I haven't had a drink since."

Her face paled even more, and she shuffled back again. He reached out his hands toward her, but she stepped back and hid her hands behind her back.

Her sudden fear cut into him like a knife. In order to push away the hurt, he turned to Susan. "I'd like to talk to your husband. Maybe I can help him. Of course, that will only happen if he wants to be helped."

"What can you do?"

"I can talk to him as someone who knows what he's going through—someone who has been there, and has overcome it. He can lean on me when he needs someone to talk to, and I can guide him when he needs guiding. I lead a small group for alcoholics who meet at my church every Saturday morning. Leaning on God and trusting in Him is the biggest source of our strength. Eric is invited to join us."

Susan didn't reply. But Lacey did.

"I thought you went to a men's group at your church on Saturday mornings."

"I do. It's for men who don't go to regular AA meetings anymore because we wanted something more God centered. We meet at my church once a week, away from the rest of the general membership. We talk, we pray and we help each other deal with issues and problems, like any other kind of support group. Other times we just take a break and do something fun—but whatever we do, everybody goes. For example, a few weeks ago we went golfing. Except I'm not really a golf fan, so I snuck in one of those exploding golf balls."

Randy's lower lip quivered, and he broke into a grin thinking of that day. He hadn't realized how completely an exploding golf ball would shatter. The whole group of them were rolling on the ground laughing long after all the dust cleared, including the guy who'd actually hit the fake golf ball. "It couldn't have been more perfect. I don't know how everyone knew it was me who brought it, but you should have seen when..." Randy let his voice trail off.

Lacey wasn't smiling. She wasn't even mildly amused.

Her voice came out in a little squeak. "You lied to me."

He could almost see the wall going up between them, brick by brick. "I didn't lie. I just didn't tell you all the details. I can tell you about myself, but I'm not supposed to tell you the exact nature of the group. Then you'd know that every one of them was an alcoholic, and that would be a breach of trust and confidentiality. I hope you'll be discreet when you meet everyone, now that you know."

"I don't even know who they are. Just that you go. Why didn't you tell me?"

"It's not the kind of thing that works its way into a normal conversation. I guess I was waiting for the right time."

More than waiting for the right time, he had been afraid to tell her. He didn't know if she'd ever seen that side of life. He knew she hadn't been a Christian all her life, but he doubted she'd ever drunk anything stronger than a glass of wine.

His fears had been accurate. Except she was taking it much worse than his imagined worst-case scenario.

He didn't know what to do.

After he got home from his stint at the drinking-and-driving public service booth on Saturday, he'd spent the rest of the day praying. Not that being at the booth made him want to take up drinking again, but just the opposite. Suddenly he'd wanted to prove to her how far away he was from the people who had come into the booth not looking for answers, but only to hear what they wanted to hear.

He needed Lacey's respect, as if that validated how far he'd grown as a human being. Lacey's opinion shouldn't have mattered any more than anyone else's, yet it did. He knew he could never be good husband material to any woman, least of all Lacey. But that didn't mean they couldn't be friends. Although, suddenly the unexpected things he was thinking about what he could do with Lacey had little to do with mere friendship.

With that thought in mind, he almost would have welcomed it if Lacey's "boyfriend" did punch his lights out, as he'd told Adrian, because then the lines would be drawn. It would have been over, and the best man would have won the fair maiden.

But Bryce wasn't her boyfriend.

Instead of drawing a firm line that he couldn't cross, from the first words they'd exchanged, Randy had felt an instant bond with Bryce, like they could become good friends.

"Do you have any more nasty secrets?"

Randy cringed. "It's not something I'm proud of, but it's not exactly a nasty secret. You're labeling me as still guilty, and I'm not. I've never been arrested, and I've never hurt anyone but myself. It hasn't cost society a lot of money to rehabilitate me with questionable results. I've done it with the help of God and my friends instead of letting it beat me down." He stared pointedly into her eyes. "So don't paint me into that corner. I pay my taxes and I'm a productive member of society. I do my best to help others not go down that same path, because I know where it can go."

She backed up until she pressed herself against the wall. "I'm sorry. I didn't mean it that way. It's just a shock to find out like this."

He stared at Lacey. Her reaction hurt him deeply. Part of him was very angry that she was judging him without giving him a chance to prove himself. But then, the reason the conversation started was because Eric was probably everything Randy used to be, except Randy had never been married.

Regardless, there were some things that all alcoholics shared. Like Randy, Eric's drinking had escalated to a point beyond his control, and he was hurting everyone around him, especially those whom he loved the most.

Thinking of Eric, Randy turned back to Susan. "I'm sorry. I forget where we were in our conversation."

Susan glanced back and forth between Lacey and Randy. "I'm the one who should be sorry. I didn't mean to cause problems between you two."

The mental picture of the perfect enabler flashed through Randy's head. "That's the second time since we've met that you've apologized for something you haven't done wrong. If you want to help your husband, the first thing you've got to do is to stop taking the blame for things you haven't done."

"But—"

He turned and extended one hand toward Lacey, looking at her while speaking to Susan. "Lacey and I haven't known each other long, but whatever happens between us won't be because of anything you've said or done. If you aren't responsible, don't apologize for something you didn't do wrong. Do you understand that?"

He turned back to Susan.

Susan nodded slowly.

He turned back to Lacey. "Can we talk about this later?"

Lacey nodded cautiously.

Randy wasn't encouraged.

Susan picked up her purse, dug through the contents for a tissue and blew her nose. "I just don't understand how you can help. Eric's drinking is ruining our marriage, but he goes out and does the same thing over and over."

"Do you think he realizes that he has a problem?"

"I'm sure he does. He's quit a number of times. If he makes a point of quitting, doesn't that mean he acknowledges something is wrong?"

Randy nodded. "That's a good start. If you two have had a big fight today, unless he's subject to blackouts, tomorrow would be a good time for me to talk to him, when he's still reeling from the effects of what he's done."

"He's got to go to work tomorrow. What about today?"

"If he's drunk now, this isn't a good time to talk. Tomorrow morning would be best, before work and before he can fall into his normal routine. If he'll talk to me tomorrow morning, I can take him out for breakfast before he goes to work."

"You would do that? You don't even know him. Or me. Why are you doing this?"

Using more courage than he had for years, Randy stepped back and reached for Lacey's hand. He intertwined their fingers, just as she had done to him before she learned of his history, and gave her hand a gentle squeeze, taking advantage of the fact that Susan was watching, making it awkward for Lacey to pull away. Again, he looked at Lacey while he spoke to Susan. "I'm doing it because I want to help anyone get out of the grip of the trap of alcohol abuse. It's what God has called me to do. You're also Lacey's sister. So that's two good reasons."

His heart pounded while he waited, but Lacey didn't pull her hand away. Even though it wasn't the best situation, and he knew he wasn't playing fair, he wasn't ready to let go of her hand. He hadn't had much physical contact in his life until he became friends with Bob's family and got to know Bob's mother. His head swam with the sensation of holding Lacey's warm hand in his.

"How will you do that?" Susan asked. "Don't you have to go to work in the morning?"

Not releasing Lacey's hand, he turned back to Susan. "Yes, but I work at the mall, so I don't have to be there until nine-fifteen. Most people are already at work by the time I'm just getting out of bed in the morning. I have plenty of time to take Eric out for breakfast."

Susan's voice shook as she spoke. "I'll phone Lacey later and let her know what Eric says. I should go. It's past time for my daughter's nap, and I really should take her home. Besides, I'm not being very good company." Susan stood and turned to leave the room, but she only took a single step, froze, then turned to Randy.

"I don't know how to thank you for what you're offering." Tears again welled up in her eyes, and she sniffled. "I don't even know your name."

Since Randy was holding Lacey's right hand with his left, he extended his free right hand and enclosed Susan's smaller hand in his own. "My name is Randy," he said. Fortunately, he didn't have to say the rest to Susan, at least not today. He'd said it so many times it was automatic in certain circles, but here he struggled with the words as he recited the next part mentally. *And I'm an alcoholic.*

He released Susan's hand so she could go home. Before she took one step, the same children who'd jumped up on Bryce earlier wrapped themselves around Susan's legs. The boy looked like he was in the first couple of years of grade school and the little girl looked like she was in preschool, which made sense if her mother said she needed a nap.

Susan smiled weakly, and twined her fingers in the little girl's hair. "These are my children, Shawn and Kaitlyn. I guess you'll probably be seeing a lot of them. Kids, this is Randy."

They clung their mother's legs, stared at his hand joined with Lacey's, then looked up at him with big, wide eyes.

"Hi, kids," Randy said, not knowing quite what to do. He liked children, but he didn't have a lot of experience with them, which, with his history, was not a bad thing. He'd messed up his own life enough.

"Come on, Shawn, Kaitlyn. It's time to go home." In the blink of an eye, the three of them were gone.

Randy turned to Lacey and gave the hand he was holding a gentle squeeze, just to remind her that they were still connected. "Should I leave, too?"

Lacey's voice came out as a rough whisper. "I don't know."

At least she was being honest, which for now was the best he could hope for.

"I'm still the same person as before, you know."

"I'm sure you are, but now I see that I don't know that person. This is so hard for me. You probably have a good idea what kind of things I've seen between Eric and Susan because of his drinking."

Over the past six years, that was exactly the reason he hadn't become involved in a relationship, but from the other side of the fence. He didn't want to be the one who would hurt the other person with his obsessive behavior. However, in offering to help Eric, he realized how far he'd come. He never had any hesitations about helping a stranger, but it was taking a lot of inner strength to step forward in a situation where he couldn't be just an anonymous mentor. This was personal, and he had something personal at stake.

"You've got to remember that I'm different than Eric."

She paused and drew in a shuddering breath. "It's not just Eric who drinks too much. My father drank, too. He died in a car accident when he was the one who was the drunk driver. Now I know why you knew so much at the booth in the mall. You're one of them."

If Randy didn't feel sick enough before, he felt worse now. He wanted to say he wasn't that bad, but he had been. There were many times he'd been out drinking and driving, and many times that he'd come very close to an accident. It was only by the grace of God that he hadn't killed someone else, or himself.

His mind reeled at the foggy memories of the one accident he'd been in, even though he wasn't the driver. It had been his twenty-fifth birthday. He'd been out to party with the guys from work, drinking more than anyone else, justifying it because it was his birthday. Randy knew he shouldn't drive, so Karl had offered to drive him home. One minute, they were laughing like idiots, and the next minute everything went black. In the end, Randy only had minor injuries, but Karl never woke up. That day had been the last time he'd had a drink.

"Please, believe me. Those days are gone for me. I don't ever want to go there again. An addiction can be hard to overcome, but not impossible. I can't say it often enough that God's grace has saved me, in more ways than I can count."

She stared at him, not saying a word.

"I want Eric to quit drinking and get to know God the same way I did. But in order for that to happen, it takes a lot of people, and a lot of support. Eric is going to need Susan behind him more than ever, and with everything going on, and all the changes, Susan's going to need you, too. In order to be of the most help, it's going to take a lot of commitment from both of us, and that means we're going to be seeing a lot of each other. We'll have to work together to help both Eric and Susan. That's the only way this is going to happen."

He waited for what felt like an eternity for Lacey's response.

"Okay," she whispered.

What Randy really wanted to do was pull Lacey close and hold her to him, which was strange because he'd never been a huggy type of person. He couldn't remember his mother ever hugging him, and certainly not his father. The last person who'd hugged him was Bob's mother on his twenty-sixth birthday, the one-year anniversary of Karl's death. He didn't know why it had happened, but at the time he'd burst into tears. He hadn't even cried at Karl's funeral. He'd felt like an idiot, but Bob's mother hadn't minded. Instead, she'd hugged him tighter, which only made him fall apart even worse. She'd told him that it was about time, and then, when he'd finally managed to get himself under control, she had said that it was time to move on with his life. She was right. The next day had been the one-year anniversary of his sobriety, and the first day of the rest of his life.

He didn't know why he really wanted to hold Lacey, because she certainly wasn't being receptive to him. He just wanted the connection. Needed it.

But whatever the reason, it was a line he couldn't cross.

Randy dropped her hand and stepped back.

Lacey quickly glanced from side to side. "I really

should get back to the party and get busy. I can't leave all this mess for Mom to clean up by herself."

"Then I should probably leave."

Lacey's face reddened. "I'm being a terrible host. I invited you so you could have a good time and meet new people, not just to help with Bryce's computer. Please go mingle, or go see what Bryce is doing. I have to go find my mom."

Randy didn't want to leave Lacey alone with her thoughts quite yet, but he liked to think he could take a hint. He nodded, and left the kitchen.

The second he entered the living room, one of Bryce's friends approached him.

"Bryce told me you know a lot about computers. My computer keeps rebooting. Do you think it might have a virus?"

A woman he hadn't met yet also joined them. "I was wondering if you could give me a little advice. I can't get my printer to work. I thought I installed it properly, but it won't even do the test page. Do you have any ideas?"

Randy mentally ran through a list of what could be wrong with both units. For now, he didn't mind giving out free technical support because it gave him something to keep his mind occupied.

Still, in the back of his mind, he couldn't help but think of Lacey. He couldn't erase the past, but there had to be something he could do to build toward the future—a future that suddenly included more than just himself.

"Hi, Lacey. Your boyfriend was right."

Lacey lowered her cell phone for a second, smiled at her customer to indicate that she would be a few minutes, then turned to the side to continue her conversation.

Good manners would have her respond to Susan's greeting, but no words would come. Randy may have been right, but Susan was wrong. Randy wasn't her boyfriend, and he would never be her boyfriend. However, Lacey didn't know what to say to Susan, because, just as Randy warned her, she didn't want to do anything to discourage Susan. Being married to Eric, Susan didn't have enough encouraging moments.

Susan kept talking, not noticing Lacey's lack of reply. "Remember when Randy said that the best time to talk to Eric wasn't when he was feeling better? When I left with the kids, he'd forgotten about Bryce's party. He thought I was leaving him, and it scared him. He'd been sick, and he wasn't fully sober when I got home, but he agreed to talk to Randy this morning. He just phoned me from work to say he was sorry about yesterday. Isn't that great?"

Lacey tried not to let her doubts about the likelihood of long-term success dampen the small bit of encouragement. If any man had treated Lacey like Eric treated Susan, Lacey would have expected more than an apologetic phone call the next day. But for Susan, an apology was better than what happened most of the times Eric did something.

"Yes, that is great," she said, trying her best to sound like she meant it.

"I don't know what Randy said, but you're so lucky to have met him. He's wonderful."

Lacey bit her lower lip. The same thing had happened at Bryce's party. The minute Randy left, everyone started talking about him, about how funny and charming and smart he was. Yet, even while everyone was enthusiastically singing Randy's praises, Randy's words *"I'm an alcoholic, too"* repeated through her head, over and over, drowning out everything good everyone was saying about him. She didn't want to be negative, but she had to be realistic. He was an alcoholic, just like Eric and just like her father.

"I hope Eric really quits this time," Lacey said quietly, for lack of anything better to say.

"I know what you're thinking."

Lacey cringed. She highly doubted Susan knew what she was thinking, because even Lacey didn't know what she was thinking.

Susan didn't wait for Lacey to respond. "You're thinking that this time isn't going to be any different from any other times. But it's going to work this time. I know it."

Lacey had heard that line before. The only thing different was that this time there was another person involved—a wild card. And Randy definitely was wild.

The image of his cheery smile and striking blue eyes flashed through her brain, even though she didn't want to think about him.

She honestly didn't know what it would be like for Randy to help Eric, if it would be difficult for him. She supposed that would depend on if Eric had only submitted because he had finally pushed Susan past her limit, or if this time he truly recognized the depth of his problems.

She wondered if the same had happened to Randy, and if there had been a woman involved.

Lacey shook her head. She already knew enough— Randy was an alcoholic. That was all she needed to know.

"Did Eric say anything about the next time he was going to see Randy?"

"No," Susan replied. "I wish I knew." Her voice dropped in pitch, and it almost sounded like she was going to start crying. "All I know is that I don't know what I would have done if Randy hadn't come along."

Lacey winced. She'd never heard Susan talk like

that before. It made her both nervous, and a failure as a sister not to have seen that things were worse than usual. She wanted to do something for Susan, something to show her that no matter what happened, she wasn't alone. Their mother never said anything, as if if she did it would be a reminder of her painful history with an alcoholic spouse.

The smart thing to do would be to talk to someone who had more experience than she did. She probably should have gone to see her pastor, but the last time Pastor Luke had talked to Eric, the visit had made Eric worse.

There really was only one person she could talk to.

Lacey turned to the right, and looked at the wall. Of course she couldn't see through it, but she knew what was behind it.

The computer store, and one computer salesman in particular.

She set her attention back to the phone. "Yes, Randy is really different, isn't he? I really should go now, Susan. After all, I am at work. I'll give you a call later, when I'm off tonight."

Lacey flipped her cell phone shut and stared at the wall.

In an hour, one of her part-time staff would be there, and she was scheduled to take a coffee break.

Today she wasn't going to take her break alone.

Chapter Five

Randy nodded at his customer. "Yes, I have one of those right here." He turned around and raised his arm, then froze, his hand resting on the box as he stared at the wall the shelf was mounted on.

Lacey was on the other side of that wall.

He couldn't help himself. He'd been thinking about her all day.

He ignored his customer and leaned closer to the wall. If he couldn't see her through the wall, maybe he could hear her voice....

"Hi, Randy. I was wondering if you were due for a coffee break?"

Randy nearly choked as he spun around.

"Lacey," he sputtered when he could find his voice. "What are you doing here?"

"I need to talk to you."

Randy's mind raced. He had the impression that talking in the store wasn't what she had in mind.

He finished his transaction, called for Carol to relieve him at the counter, then accompanied Lacey to the food court.

The second they were seated at a table, Randy raised one palm toward her so he could speak first.

"I hope you know that whatever is said between me and Eric stays between me and Eric. Everything remains confidential. There can be no exceptions."

"But he's married to my sister!"

"That doesn't matter."

Her expression immediately conveyed that she felt betrayed.

Randy cradled his cup in his hands and leaned back into the chair. He wanted nothing more than for Lacey to trust him but, for now, Eric's needs were more important than Randy's wants. "You have to understand something. What I'm doing with him is highly confidential. It's just like if you said something really personal to your pastor. You'd expect it never to be repeated to anyone, at any time, for any reason. It's a matter of trust. If that trust isn't there, then this won't work. This is new for him, and he's going to have to make some major changes in his attitudes, and his life. When he's ready to share with other people, he will. And when that happens isn't up to me."

She stared at him, her eyes wider than he'd ever seen. "Is that how you did it?"

Randy's chest tightened. "There was an older man who helped me along until I could be on my own and start offering help to others. I told him many things I never even told Bob, my best friend. It's a unique relationship, and one that involves a lot of trust. And responsibility."

"Oh."

He wanted to say more, but he couldn't. He wanted to show her how much he'd changed and grown, to show her the man he'd become, versus the pathetic drunk he'd once been. But then, the only way to know the difference was to tell her exactly how pathetic he once was, and he wasn't going to do that. By God's grace, that person no longer existed. Instead, he would show her the man he was today.

"I was going to ask if you would come to the Bible study meeting with me tonight, but I can't go. I'm seeing Eric, instead."

He held his breath, waiting, hoping she was going to say something about driving him home from work.

Lacey stood. "I think our break is up."

Randy stood so quickly he almost spilled the remainder of his coffee. "Will I see you after work?"

Her hesitation nearly killed him. "You need a ride home, don't you?"

"Yes." He waited for her to say more, but she

didn't. She hadn't said, "no" so he took it as a "yes." They walked back in silence until they reached Randy's store.

Randy rammed his hands into his pockets. "Do you want to stop for dinner on the way home?"

"I thought you were going out with Eric."

"Not for supper. He needs to spend time with his family. I'm going to pick him up at seven o'clock, then go to the meeting after that."

"I wonder if I should go to be with Susan while he's gone."

"That probably wouldn't be a bad idea. Except I want to take my car tonight. How about if after dinner you take me to my place, I'll pick up my car, then I'll follow you to your place to drop off your car, and we can go to Eric and Susan's together. Then when we're done with Eric and Susan, maybe the two of us can go out for coffee afterward."

"That sounds so complicated."

"It probably is, but for now it's important to take my car because it demonstrates to Eric who's in charge. It's kind of a guy-power thing. Tonight if we're in my car, that puts me in charge. It's harder to create that mental image of authority if he's driving me around in his car. It's not going to be such a big issue later, but for the first time, it's important to create a pecking order, for lack of a better name to call it."

"I suppose that makes sense. I guess I'll see you later."

Before she could change her mind, Randy turned into his store, and went back to work.

Lacey bit into the doughnut, then dabbed at the powdered sugar on her lips with her napkin. "I can't remember the last time I've been out this late on a weeknight."

Randy licked a dribble of jam off his lips, then swiped the back of his hand across his mouth. "It's not that late. Neither of us has to get up for work at dawn or anything. I get up at eight o'clock, and I still have plenty of time to get ready in the morning. What about you?"

"I guess I get up about the same time."

Lacey looked around the doughnut shop, desperately needing to talk about something else. She didn't want to think of him doing the same things at the same time as she did in the morning. "I can't remember the last time I was inside a doughnut shop. I always get a selection at the drive-thru window and keep going. But here, they all know you. And you know them, without needing to read their name tags."

"Yeah, well, you know how it goes."

She didn't really, but she nodded anyway. Although it did make sense. On the surface, Randy was an easy person to like. The second they'd walked in, every one of the staff members stopped what they were doing and smiled. Every one of them greeted him personally, and he cheerfully greeted them all back, calling them all individually by name. He'd even winked at one of the younger girls, who'd giggled and blushed profusely before returning to work, smiling long after Randy stopped paying her attention.

"You do the same thing at my store. I can't believe they all know you."

"That's 'cause I'm such a handsome and dashing kinda guy."

Unfortunately, all her staff thought exactly that, too. All work stopped when Randy walked into the store to ask if she was ready to take her break.

"That's because you're the only man who dares to walk into a ladies' boutique unescorted. You're also a flirt."

He winked, grinned, splayed one hand over his heart, then fluttered his long eyelashes.

Lacey nearly choked on her doughnut. "Stop it. Don't you ever quit fooling around?"

He lowered his hand. "I can be very serious when I need to be."

Lacey wiped her lips again. "I guess you can. Speaking of serious, how did things go with Eric?"

"Good." Randy took another bite of his doughnut. "Their kids are sure cute. They have a nice house, too, but did you see your nephew's bedroom? I could barely tell what color the carpet was. It was buried at least a couple of inches deep in cars, action figures, building blocks and used socks."

"I can barely believe how quickly you managed to change the subject."

All he did was shrug his shoulders. He didn't deny her statement.

"It's not always that bad," Lacey said, deciding to go with the change in subject. "But it is usually messy. No matter how hard Susan tries, she can't seem to keep up. I know Bryce's room was never tidy. I think all boys are like that."

"I always kept my room clean."

"What about your brothers or sisters?"

"I was an only child."

Once again, she waited for him to say more about his family, but he didn't. She wanted to know more, but Randy was always so closemouthed about family situations. The only thing he had told her was that for a while he lived off and on with his best friend's family. Even then, he hadn't been very forthcoming with details.

Eric had a few brothers and a sister, yet she did remember that he hadn't wanted to have children, and he hadn't been in a rush to get married. In both cases, it was only because of Susan's insistence, which, even then, Lacey hadn't thought was a good idea.

"Susan told me she wants to have another baby to have three kids, just like our family."

Randy picked up his coffee mug, cradling it in his hands, and leaned back in his chair. "The couple down the hall from me just had a baby. It's their second child. I don't know what they're doing up there on the seventeenth floor. You'd figure they would move into a house, like Susan and Eric. That's the way I always thought it should be. You know. Room to do ball games in the backyard. Have a dog or some kind of pet." He shrugged his shoulders. "But then my parents had a house and we had everything that went with it. Except the dog. They wouldn't let me have a dog. I once thought that would be the answer for everything." He set his mug back on the table. "Do you want more coffee? They make a special blend I just love. Sometimes I buy it by the pound and make this coffee at home."

Without waiting for her to respond, Randy turned and signaled the waiter.

Lacey felt stunned. She had a feeling that he'd just said something deeply personal, but she wasn't quite sure what it was. Then, as he always did when personal issues came up, he'd changed the subject so quickly she didn't have time to think about what he'd said, or respond to it.

This time she couldn't let it go. Her mind raced as she tried to think of something appropriate to say.

"Kaitlyn wants a dog really bad, but Susan doesn't trust Eric to look after a dog properly. Puppies are a lot of work."

"I agree with her on that. It's also more than just a care issue. There's a good chance that a dog would become Eric's drinking buddy. Alcoholics sometimes treat pets that way. If I would have had a dog, I don't know if it would have ended up being my drinking buddy. Maybe it's just as well it didn't happen."

Again, Lacey was stunned by the wisdom of Randy's words. Yet, his insights still didn't change the fact that he'd been an alcoholic—he was just being more honest about it than either her father or Eric.

His expression turned thoughtful. "Bob never had a dog, but once he did have a pair of hamsters. Do you know how fast those things multiply? I was going to say that they multiply like rabbits, but really, a rabbit's reputation to multiply far exceeds reality. Actually, rabbits are supposed to make good house pets. Some can be litter-box trained, but I'd still rather have a dog."

It took Lacey a few seconds to switch her train of thought. She had never known someone who changed the subject so quickly, or was so adept at it. The scariest part was that she could follow him. "Are you always like this?"

"Like what?"

Lacey stood. "Never mind. I think it's time to go."

They chatted during the trip home, but the closer they came to Lacey's apartment building, the more conversation began to lapse.

She didn't know why she wasn't surprised when Randy parked his car in the visitor parking area and walked her to the door. When she unlocked the main door, he followed her inside, as if he didn't consider the possibility that once they made it to her apartment, she wouldn't invite him in.

All the way up the elevator, there was only silence.

She unlocked her apartment door and opened it, but he didn't move.

She turned around to face him, not sure if she should bid him farewell or actually invite him in.

Randy spoke first, saving her the decision.

"I'm not going to go in—it's getting late enough—but I couldn't say this in the doughnut shop. I feel some tension between us, and there shouldn't be. I want you to know that I'm fine. For the days I don't feel fine, then God helps me. There's a verse in Second Timothy that says 'Yet, I am not ashamed, because I know whom I have believed, and am convinced that He is able to guard what I have entrusted to Him for that day.' So because I'm trusting God to keep my life on track, as they say in AA, one day at a time, I'm asking you to trust me, too."

Trust.

Lacey didn't know how such a short word could carry so much power, or ask so much.

His voice deepened, lowering in both pitch and volume. "I'm still the same person as I was on Sunday morning, before you knew."

"I know," she said softly, the words almost hard to say. He was that same person. What she didn't know was how well she knew that person. Yet, for all her hesitations, he'd done nothing wrong so far. All she could think of were the verses she'd read where God cautioned His children to stay away from drunkards. Even though Randy hadn't had a drink for a few years, he freely admitted to having a problem with alcohol, so it still counted. God's advice was good. She knew from close experience the heartache of being married to an alcoholic, both during marriage, and after it was yanked away and all that was left was a gaping hole and continued losses.

He reached forward and grasped one of her hands, then massaged her wrist gently with his thumb. "I'm seeing Eric again tomorrow evening, but it's going to be an early meeting. Can we have a quick dinner together, so we can do the same thing as tonight?"

"I don't know if I should."

"I'll pay."

Lacey scrambled to think of an excuse. "No. This

must be getting so expensive for you. We've been out for supper so many times, and you've only let me pay once."

"I let you pay twice."

"I had a coupon. That didn't count."

Randy smiled at her comeback. "Then I have an idea. We won't have much time, anyway, so how about if we throw something quick together at my place and keep going? At work, I often grab a quick burger for lunch. I hate doing that for supper, too. But I can make something better at home, and then we can go straight to Eric and Susan's place together."

"But…" Lacey let her voice trail off. That wasn't what she meant. She certainly wasn't fishing for an invitation, but now that he'd invited her, she didn't know how to back out graciously, especially since he was doing so much to help her brother-in-law.

"I'm a good cook. Promise."

"Am I going to be able to come up with a reason why this isn't a good idea?"

"I hope not."

She looked up into Randy's face, into his beautiful blue eyes, which radiated only hope and sincerity. Her heart told her that so far he'd done nothing wrong. In fact, he'd done everything right. But the more sensible part of her couldn't trust him because of what he had been.

"You're taking too long to answer. You're making me nervous."

His words made her chest tighten. She wasn't being fair to Randy, and she knew it, but she couldn't stop the way she felt. She knew she shouldn't sit in judgment, and she probably owed him the chance to prove himself. Besides, just because she went to his home for dinner, that didn't mean she was obligated to spend the rest of eternity with him.

"I'm sorry. Yes, that would be nice."

"Great. I'll see you tomorrow. Good night."

He turned and left before she had a chance to change her mind.

"Wow. Something smells good."

Randy walked into the kitchen, with Lacey following behind. "It's not a big deal. I do this all the time. I just put a bunch of stuff in the slow cooker in the morning, and when I get home, it magically turns into beef stew."

She lifted the lid of the slow cooker, peeked inside and inhaled deeply. "It looks as good as it smells, too."

Randy opened the cupboard door and began to set the table.

He didn't know why it was important to him, but he wanted to show Lacey what God had done in his life. After being with Eric a few times, Randy was getting a good idea of what she'd seen, and it hadn't been good. Randy wanted her to see that he would never, ever be like Eric as she now knew him.

Not that he could ever be someone he wasn't, but he wanted to show her that he could be someone she could at least like.

Randy straightened the place settings, and turned to Lacey. "When I stayed with Bob's family, I used to spend a lot of time in the kitchen with his mother, and his brother, Tony. Everyone in that family cooks. In fact, Tony even opened up his own restaurant."

Bob's mother had taught him well the value of a well-prepared meal. Also, by being with Bob's family, he'd learned that there was more to a meal than just eating. For them, taking the time to be together with family and friends was often more important than the food. When he moved out, it had been a huge adjustment to eat alone. Now that he'd been with Lacey for dinner so many days in a row, something inside him ached at the thought of going back to dinner-for-one.

Randy placed two glasses on the table. "Everything is done, so this will be even faster than grabbing a burger, and way more nutritious. I don't think we have time to make dumplings. I hope that's okay."

"Dumplings? You make dumplings? Yourself?"

He unplugged the slow cooker and carried it to the table rather than putting the stew into a bowl, so he'd have less dishes to wash. "I told you I was a good cook. Didn't you believe me?" They sat down at the table.

Her cheeks flushed. "I'm sorry. I thought you were just joking. I don't know what to say."

"How about saying grace?"

Lacey immediately led with a short prayer, and they began to eat.

Randy watched as she took her first mouthful. She closed her eyes and chewed slowly, savoring the flavor. "This is so good."

He shrugged his shoulders. "I like to eat, so I'd better be a good cook."

Lacey savored another mouthful before she spoke again. "You must have done a lot of cooking when you were a kid."

"No. I didn't." The truth was, no matter what he did, it was never good enough, and that included his feeble attempts at cooking. "But I did a lot of cooking with Bob's family over the years. There were six kids in that family. Before the first one got married, including Bob's parents, that was nine people to feed at every meal, more if they had other guests besides me." He smiled at some of the memories from Bob's mother's kitchen. "Mealtime was a real family affair over there, always very interactive. Bob's mother made sure everyone had a job to do. If you ate, you were expected to work. She has a Bible verse on the kitchen wall, saying so. Sometimes, though, I think that organizing everyone and acting as referee was harder work than if she would have just done everything herself. I learned a lot from Bob's mom."

"She sounds like a very special lady."

"She is." Randy sucked in a deep breath. "If you want to meet her of course she'll be at the wedding, which is in a couple of weeks. Want to come with me? I can introduce you then."

Lacey's fork froze in midair. "Pardon me?"

"I'm going to be Bob's best man. Would you like to come as my guest? I'd be honored if you'd accompany me."

Her eyes widened as she stared at him. Every second felt like an hour.

"I guess I can. Is it going to be a large wedding?"

"Up until last weekend we thought it was just going to be Bob's family, but I heard talk that George's family is thinking of coming after all."

Lacey's eyes widened even more. "George?"

Randy grinned. "The bride-to-be. Her name is really Georgette, but everyone calls her George. It's a long story. I'll tell it to you someday." His smile deepened as he thought of Bob and George's courtship, most of which was spent under the hoods of various cars, or taking apart Bob's old motorcycle and putting it back together again in Bob's driveway on the weekends.

Randy hadn't done a lot of dating, but he'd always pictured something more romantic—like soft music, fragrant flowers and a cozy table for two in a classy, expensive fine restaurant.

His smile dropped as the reality of his messy kitchen, the not-soothing sound of a siren in addition to the noise of the regular city traffic echoing up through the window, and his not-so-famous everyday crockpot stew, without the dumplings, sunk in.

"Randy? Is something wrong?"

He shook his head. "No. But we should get going soon. Eric is expecting me. I don't want to be late."

Lacey checked her watch. "You're right. I was thinking… Rather than go to Eric and Susan's house in one car, we should both take our own cars from here."

"But that doesn't make any sense."

"It makes a lot of sense. We don't have time tonight to drop my car off at my place, and that way I won't have to come all the way here and then drive all the way home. It will save time late at night to just go home from their place."

"I don't know." Randy didn't like the idea, and the more he thought about it, the more he realized why. He didn't want to go their separate ways from Eric and Susan's house. He wanted to have some kind of private goodbye moment with Lacey when the evening was over, maybe even ending with a good-night kiss.

Randy shook his head. He didn't know where that thought had come from. It wasn't like he'd never kissed a woman before. But he'd never planned it in advance.

Ever since the day he'd met Lacey, he'd felt like someone had taken his life, put it in a bag and then turned it upside down and shaken it.

He didn't know why he'd just invited Lacey to Bob and George's wedding. It just felt right. Even with all his uncertainty, he felt strangely relieved, even happy, that she'd be accompanying him, even though being together at a friend's wedding was a more intimate affair than just sharing a ride home and a meal on the way.

He wondered if Lacey cried at weddings. At Adrian and Celeste's wedding, Randy had found himself getting a little choked up, but he'd told himself that it was because Adrian, Bob, Paul and he had been inseparable for years. And now Bob was cutting loose.

As he thought of what was in store at Bob's wedding, standing up at the front in the hallowed position of best man, he thought of his friendship with Bob, who had been with him at the best times in his life and the worst. Randy wondered if he'd be crying at Bob's wedding, too.

Was it acceptable to wear sunglasses in church?

"That was great. Thank you so much. Can I help you clean up?"

Randy blinked as he dragged his brain back to the present. "Sure."

Lacey stacked the plates in the sink while Randy

dumped the leftover stew into a plastic container and put it in the fridge.

"I'll do the dishes later. Let's go."

Lacey raised her fist to knock on Susan's door, but the door opened before she made contact.

She stepped back so she wouldn't whack her sister in the head.

"Susan? Have you been crying? What's wrong?"

Asking the question was merely a formality. Lacey already knew she wouldn't have to wait for Susan's reply to hear what was wrong.

Eric.

He'd done something. Again.

After he'd promised to quit drinking.

Again.

Lacey stepped inside, with Randy right behind her, and closed the door.

Susan sniffled. "I'm so scared. Eric didn't come home from work. He said he was going out with his usual drinking buddies. He promised me he was only going to have one and then come home because he was supposed to be going out with Randy. But it's been three hours, and he's still not here." Tears began to roll down her cheeks. "He promised me this was it, that he was going to change. Today was payday. He's got his whole paycheck in his pocket."

Words failed Lacey. She couldn't tell Susan that

she'd had doubts from the beginning in Eric's ability to reform, despite Randy's involvement and help. All week long she'd felt guilty for her uncertainty, but she was only being realistic. Now, only a few days later, the reason for her doubts had come to pass. Not only that, but they remembered from their childhood what happened every payday.

Guilt washed through her that instead of being there for her sister, she'd been at Randy's apartment, enjoying a surprisingly good home-cooked supper.

"You should have called me. I could have come sooner."

"I tried, but I only got your voice mail, so I didn't leave a message. I don't have Randy's number."

Lacey fished through her purse for her cell phone. "Ugh. The battery is dead. I didn't hear the warning beep. I'm so sorry. But we're here now. I wish there was something I could do."

Randy stepped forward. "There's nothing you can do, but there is something I can do." He turned to Susan. "If you tell me where he is, I'll go see what I can do to get him to come home. He probably feels pretty guilty, knowing he's failed again, which makes him drink more. Then the more he drinks, the worse he feels, which makes him drink even more, and then he feels even worse and the cycle continues. It's a real downward spiral and it's not rational, but often that's the way it goes."

"If you go to the bar, what can you do?"

Randy shrugged his shoulders. "I'm not sure. At best, I'm hoping I can bring him home and he can sleep it off, and we'll talk tomorrow. At the very least, I want to make sure he doesn't drive home." He reached into his pocket for his keys. "If you tell me where he is, I'll be on my way."

Susan sniffled again, and swiped her nose with the back of her hand. "He's at the hotel at the corner of Fifth and Main."

Lacey spun around to face him. "You're going into a bar? Where there's drinking?"

"If that's where he is, that's where I have to go in order to get him. He's not going to come to me if I stand on the street corner and call him."

"But…" Lacey let her voice trail off. She didn't want to ask her question, yet it was something that had to be addressed.

Randy beat her to the draw. He held up one hand to silence her. "I know what you're thinking. I would be fooling myself if I said I would be able to sit down with him, just have one drink and then I would stop and everything would be just fine. I probably could stop after only one drink today, but then I'd be too tempted to do it again. Only, the next time, since I handled one okay, then I'd have two. And the next time I'd have three. And so on, and so on, and soon my life would be as out of control as it was before. I won't go down that road, Lacey. I know where it leads, and I don't ever want to be there again. The only way this works isn't by moderation. It's by total abstinence. Now if you'll excuse me."

He turned and left before Lacey had a chance to respond.

Again, Susan swiped at her nose with the back of her hand. "He's so brave. And so smart. You're really lucky to have him."

Lacey wasn't sure there was much difference between the definitions of bravery and foolhardiness. Most of the time, the choice of which word to use came after the fact, after everyone knew if the results of someone's efforts had met with success, or tragedy. The difference between genius and insanity was often a line the width of a hair, and she didn't know which side of the hair Randy was on.

She also didn't think luck had anything to do with her relationship with Randy. She couldn't decide if knowing him was a blessing, or a curse. Part of her couldn't help but like him, but the greater part of her was terrified.

She was almost sure that Randy would handle himself honorably with Eric, but she did worry about how going into a bar would affect Randy personally. She didn't know if hanging out at the bar was part of his former ways and he missed that part of his social life, or if he had been more solitary. Although knowing him now, the way he was, she doubted Randy had ever been solitary.

Lacey shook her head and pushed thoughts of Randy out of her head. Thinking about him only served to drive her crazy. Right now she needed to console her sister.

Lacey started walking toward the kitchen, and as she knew would happen, Susan followed her. "How about if we make some tea?" Lacey asked over her shoulder. "Where are the kids?"

"They're in their rooms. They've already eaten, and they're playing a bit before I put them to bed. I knew Eric wouldn't be home for supper, but I had no idea this was going to happen. I don't know what to do."

"All I can say is to listen to what Randy says. He's been through it, and he's okay now." She wanted with all her heart to believe her own words, but she also believed that this time Eric was really trying, too. Eric had so much to lose, but he couldn't seem to free himself from the bonds of alcohol addiction.

By the time the tea was ready, they had put the children to bed. Without the children awake, the house was totally quiet, something that didn't happen very often at Eric and Susan's house. But that wasn't necessarily a good thing. Tonight, too much silence would give Susan too much time to think. Therefore, Lacey did her best to occupy Susan's thoughts by chattering more than she'd ever chattered in her whole life, mostly about nothing important. She jumped subjects so often, she didn't know how she got from one topic to another, something she recognized as one of Randy's habits that was apparently rubbing off on her. However, she did obtain the desired result, which was to keep Susan too distracted to worry about her husband and what he could be doing right now.

The only thing that stopped her from more incessant talking was the sound of loud male voices at the front door.

The door opened. Susan froze. Eric walked in the door, with Randy behind him. Eric froze at the sight of Susan.

Lacey's stomach rolled. She didn't want to be a part of the coming unpleasant conversation.

Eric walked shakily to the recliner, where he sank down. Randy remained standing in the entrance to the living room.

Eric's voice came out in a hoarse croak, not slurred, but not quite right, either. "I'm sorry," he muttered.

"Keep going," Randy prompted him quietly.

Eric lowered his head, staring pointedly at his shoes instead of facing Susan. "I really thought I could control myself. I didn't mean it."

Susan gulped. "It's…" Her voice trailed off. Still in the doorway, Randy frantically began shaking his head and waving his arms in the air, then pressed one finger over his lips, while Eric continued to stare down at his own feet.

Susan closed her mouth and waited.

"Go on, Eric," Randy said gently, yet forcibly at the same time.

"I thought I could do it, but I can't. I really do need help. I couldn't control myself. I was going to tell Randy that I didn't want to go to any AA meetings, that I could control it, I could have just a few and leave, but I can't." He rested his elbows on his thighs, hunched over and covered his face with hands. "I can't go on like this. But I don't want anyone I know to see me. I'll go to the meetings, but I can't face anyone I know—at least not yet. If I have to go to church, I'll go to Randy's, where we don't know anyone."

Randy's eyebrows rose. "Are you sure? This is the time when you need your friends the most. I don't know if I would be where I am today if it hadn't been for my friends."

Eric shook his head, not dropping his hands from in front of his face. "I don't have any friends left. They all hate me for what I'm doing to my wife and my family, and I can't say I blame them. I have to make a clean break, and a fresh start. Starting tomorrow. I'll go back to our church when I've got everything under control."

Susan opened her mouth to speak, but no words

came out. Because Susan tended to excuse everything Eric did, Lacey had the feeling that Susan was about to say that her friends didn't hate him, but Lacey knew that was wrong. Most of their friends had stopped hanging out with them because they didn't want Eric to be a bad influence on their children. In some deep, underlying way, Eric probably knew it, and Susan wouldn't admit it.

"But it will be so hard to leave our church. All my friends go there."

Lacey reached over and rested her hand on Susan's shoulder. "It's okay. If you want, I can change churches and go to Randy's church with you, so you will have someone there. I've already been to Randy's church, and it's very nice and very friendly."

Susan gulped. "You'd do that for me?"

"Of course I would. I'm your sister."

She didn't want to think that seeing Randy on Sunday would mean she was going to be spending time with him seven days a week. She already saw him Saturdays after the morning meeting.

Randy's voice interrupted her thoughts.

"I think it's time to leave, Lacey. Eric and Susan have a lot to talk about."

"Of course." She turned to Susan. "We'll see ourselves out."

The second they were outside, Lacey looked down

the block, first to the right, then to the left. "Where's your car?" she asked.

"I left it at the hotel. I wasn't going to let Eric drive, so I relieved him of his keys, and I drove Eric's car. Now I need you to give me a ride back to the hotel, so I can pick up my car. Apparently, it was a good thing we did bring both cars tonight."

They slid into her car naturally. It had already been commonplace for her to provide transportation for Randy every day after work. She thought back to the man she'd dated before she met Randy. Jason had always insisted on driving, even when they were using her car, a trait she found annoying and even insulting.

Beside her, more than comfortable in the passenger's seat, Randy rolled the window down, fastened his seat belt and leaned back, linking his fingers behind his head. "To Fifth and Main, James," he quipped, grinning.

Lacey pretended to be annoyed, but Randy only snickered.

They had only gone a few blocks, and Lacey's mood turned very serious. "I don't know if it was such a good idea to have Eric make all those promises. He was obviously drunk. Is he going to mean it tomorrow? Do you think he's going to follow through this time?"

"Yes, I think he's finally ready. What he's done is actually pretty common. When a lot of men decide to quit drinking, knowing it's gotten to that point of no return, they get nervous about how much work it's going to be. They tell themselves they can control it, then go out intending to have just one, except that never happens. That's the time they drink more than usual because it scares them to realize the hold alcohol has on them. They can't stop. Yes, Eric was drunk, but I got to him soon enough. He wasn't incoherent. His thinking processes are clouded, but not nonexistent. He's quite capable of making the decision to do what it takes to sober up and stay sober." Randy lowered his hands from behind his head, and turned toward Lacey.

"I didn't prompt him about changing churches, I don't know where that idea came from. I just told him that if he finally can admit he has a problem he can't control alone, it was time to talk to his wife about it, deal with it, and work out some compromises together. I told him that Susan would do anything to help him through this. That's all I said."

Lacey let his words sink in, and Randy gave her the time she needed to think about it. "I believe you. But I do have something else to ask you. If it's none of my business, just say so."

"Go ahead."

"Was it hard for you to go into the bar? Did you feel like sitting down with the men and having a few drinks with them?"

"I was a little nervous. It's the first time I've been in a barroom for over six years. But once I walked inside, I realized my perspective has changed. I no longer see it as a fun way to spend the evening. I know the problems the lifestyle can cause. Once I had a look at the men Eric was with, I could also tell that it wasn't only Eric who has a serious problem, which is probably why those guys hang together. I didn't want to join them. I only wanted to get back out. I told you before, I won't go down that road again. God pulled me out, and I'm staying out."

Lacey's thoughts raced in a million directions, wanting to believe him but being too afraid. She'd heard the same kind of comments from Eric after his last big binge. Eric always said he'd learned his lesson, that he was reformed. Yet his grand promises never lasted long. She suspected the reason had a lot to do with his ego. Eric had always needed to impress people, and the alcohol seemed to help him feel important.

Lacey always thought that Susan might have done better to help Eric quit if she understood why he drank, and the reason Lacey saw was a means to bolster Eric's weak personality. However, if Eric impressed anyone, it was only the other drunks.

Which caused her to wonder why Randy drank, or rather, why he once drank. Randy didn't seem to have any problem with weakness. He definitely wasn't shy. Everything he did was bold and confident. He certainly didn't seem to worry about what others thought of him, like Eric did. Randy liked everybody, despite their faults, and everybody liked Randy. He was easy to get along with, and fun. He certainly wasn't dull or unintelligent.

Yet there had to be something, she thought, because everyone had to have a reason to drink excessively. If she could figure out why Randy once drank, she would also know when he would be prone to craving it once again. Then she would be able to do something about it, to help steer him away from temptation before he fell to it. Then, at least a little bit, she could be safe.

Until then, she knew that the thought of him sliding back into a lifestyle of drinking would continue to haunt her.

Before she had a chance to consider any more possibilities, she saw Randy's car in the parking lot and pulled in beside it.

The roar of the loud music from the bar reached them, even from the distance of the parking lot. A group of men were standing outside, near the main entrance, talking and laughing much too loudly. Toward the rear of the building another man stood alone, with his back to everyone else, facing a tree. Lacey didn't want to think of what he was doing.

The place and the atmosphere gave her the willies.

She turned to Randy as he reached for the door handle, preparing to exit the car.

She struggled to keep her voice clear and even. "I didn't want to say this before, but when you were gone, I was worried about you."

His movements froze, and he turned his head to face her. Lacey expected an impish grin and a lame joke that would lighten the moment, but his expression was the most serious she'd ever seen.

"I don't know whether that's good or bad."

"I don't know, either. I'm so confused. And so scared. This is moving too fast for me."

He reached forward and grasped her hands in his. "It's okay. I know you're out of your comfort zone. We'll just take things slow. No rush, no pressure. The only thing I ask is that you trust me."

Before she realized what he was doing, Randy tipped his head slightly, leaned forward and brushed a slow, gentle kiss to her lips. He started to move away, but then he sighed, tipped his head a little more and kissed her again—longer, fully and more firmly. When he broke away, he moved so slowly that Lacey could feel the ever-lightening sensation of his breath on her mouth as they separated. When she finally opened her eyes his were already opened. She couldn't do anything other than stare into the blue depths. As soon as it dawned on him that she was looking at him, he straightened and he quickly slid out of the car. "I'll see you tomorrow morning. I hope you have some good sidewalks on sale. I know I will."

She barely caught on to his skewed reference to the mall's sidewalk sale that was starting the next morning. In that split second it took her to figure it out, the door closed and he was gone.

She watched numbly as Randy opened his car door, waved, slipped into his car and drove off without taking any time to let the engine warm up.

Lacey would indeed see him tomorrow. And the day after that. And the day after that.

She pressed her fingers to her lips, still moist from Randy's kiss, and hoped and prayed she was doing the right thing.

Chapter Six

"A little more to the left."

"Like this?"

"Yeah, that's great."

Randy stepped back and examined the positioning of the table containing his store's featured items, priced and ready for the sidewalk sale.

Once he was assured that his own table was straight and centered, he left Carol to her arrangements of the sale merchandise and he sauntered next door.

When he was one step inside the opening to Lacey's store, he called out, "Do any lovely ladies in here need a tall, dark, handsome man to help move your table?"

The voices coming from behind one of the racks went silent. He heard the sound of muffled giggling, followed by a "Shh!"

Lacey appeared holding a bright red T-shirt, her cheeks the cutest shade of pink. "We'd love your help." She turned and handed the T-shirt to the person Randy still couldn't see, and stepped forward. The giggling started again, and didn't stop when Lacey narrowed her eyes and glared at the hidden giggler.

Randy turned toward the table, which had only a few items piled on it.

"Don't say anything," Lacey grumbled. "I made a list of things we were going to feature, but instead of piling everything up on the table, the girl who came in last night put the sale prices on everything on the list, then put everything back on the racks. As you can guess, we're way behind trying to find everything that was marked down."

Randy dragged the table outside the door, then set everything into piles as Lacey and her helper frantically tossed the sale items at him as they found them.

When Lacey stopped to throw yet another pile of clothing onto the table, Randy turned to her. "I'm working my store's table today. Are you?"

"Yes. I wasn't going to, but after you told me about the chronic shoplifters, I didn't want to put anyone too inexperienced up here. Thanks for the tip."

"You're more than welcome. I was wondering—" The sound of voices echoed from down the mall. "Oops. Time's up. I have to go," Randy said as he glanced toward the encroaching early-bird shoppers. "I'll catch you later."

He jogged the ten steps to his own table, ready for the start of what he knew would be a busy week with the sidewalk sale.

All morning, despite the constant flow of shoppers, his thoughts kept drifting to Lacey. In past years he'd always enjoyed working the sidewalk sale, but this time, he only wanted the day to be over so he could be with Lacey, with no shoppers interrupting them.

When lunchtime approached, he pulled out his cell phone and pushed his favorite sequence of numbers. He smiled when Lacey reached into her pocket and pulled out her cell phone.

"Hi," he crooned. "Is it lunchtime soon?"

She moved her cell phone away from her ear, stared at it, blinked, then turned her head and stared at him.

Randy waved. "Are we on for lunch?" he asked loudly enough to be heard from where he was standing.

She lifted the phone and spoke into it. "Are you crazy?"

From the distance, he watched her, studied her. Maybe he was crazy, but all he could think of was their parting last night—how he'd kissed her, and how he wanted to kiss her again.

"Only about you," he whispered into the phone, his voice far more husky than he meant it to be.

She stared at him, right into his face. He was almost positive that her gaze flickered to his mouth, like she was thinking the same thing he was.

Suddenly she stiffened, and she glanced at the crowd of ladies who were picking through the pile of T-shirts on her sale table.

Lacey turned her back to him so she was facing the ladies. "It's cute when you flirt with the young girls in the doughnut shop, but you're supposed to be working. Quit fooling around."

He forced his thoughts back to the throng of people at his table. "Sorry, I shouldn't have done that. Seriously, I have to tell Carol when she can take her break."

"Anna says she's hungry, so I'm going to let her go first."

"Okay. I'll tell Carol to go now."

They pushed the "end" buttons at exactly the same time. Instead of clipping the phone back on his belt, Randy hit Carol's number and told her to go for lunch.

He didn't know if it was the rain, or the season, or just plain luck for the mall management, but the crowds didn't die down after the usual lunch-hour rush. Carol only took enough time to eat, as did Anna. When Randy and Lacey arrived at the food court, every seat and every bench was full, and other people with full trays were also looking for someplace to sit down.

Lacey stood on one foot, and rubbed the top of her other foot up the side of her calf. "This is going to be the only chance I have to sit down all day. I don't want to stand during my lunch break."

Randy nodded. "I know what you mean. My store has a small table and a couple of chairs in the corner of the stock room. It's not very classy, and it's a little cramped, but it's a private place to sit down for a few minutes when everything else is nuts."

"That sounds like an offer I can't refuse."

As soon as they purchased their lunches, they returned to the computer store. Carol watched every step they took as Randy guided Lacey into the back room with him. Fortunately, Carol remained silent for one of the few times in her life.

Randy walked straight to the table, but good manners dictated that he stand and wait for Lacey to sit first.

Lacey didn't sit. All she did was stand and stare at him while he stared at her. They were so close, he could almost have leaned forward and kissed her again, just like he'd been thinking about for the past few hours.

As if she could read his mind, Lacey backed up a step.

He forced himself to look at her eyes, and not at her mouth. "I'm sorry about calling you on your cell at work earlier. I was out of line. We don't have a lot of time. Let's just sit down and relax while we can. It's going to be a long day, and a long week."

Obediently, Lacey sank down into one of the chairs and stretched her legs out in front of her. "I'm sorry, I guess I overreacted. I probably needed this break more than I thought I did. By the time the weekend gets here, I'll be wiped. None of my friends can understand what it's like to stand all day, especially when a sale is on."

Randy sank down into the other chair. He said a short prayer of thanks for their food and began to unwrap the sandwich he'd bought. He'd probably been overreacting, too, but he couldn't erase the memories of kissing Lacey.

"I know what you mean. I spend a fortune on good shoes, but when there's a sale like this, it gets me, too. By the time the week is over, I know I'll be canceling my plans just to go sit in the hot tub at my apartment complex to try to get the stiffness out."

Lacey sighed. "That must be nice."

Randy sighed back. "It is. I don't know what I would do without that hot tub. Wait. I have an idea. You'll probably be feeling just the same. Care to join me?"

"No."

Randy tried not to cringe at her instantaneous rejection of his invitation.

He didn't know if his expression gave his thoughts away, because Lacey reached over the small table and rested her hand on his arm. Her touch short-circuited his brain, making him want to lean forward and kiss her again. For the second time he pushed the thoughts from his mind.

"I'm sorry," Lacey murmured, "I didn't mean to be so abrupt. It's just that I don't want you to see me in a bathing suit."

He blinked. "Why not? Don't tell me you think you're overweight."

Her cheeks darkened, giving him his answer.

Randy's jaw tightened. Lacey wasn't exactly fashion-magazine thin, but she looked healthy. "I don't know why you're embarrassed. I watch you eat every day. I think it's great that you don't pick at your food and waste half the plate."

He looked into her face to get some hint of what she was thinking, but as usual, he got distracted, staring into her eyes. In the cramped quarters of the storage room, he was closer than usual, giving him ample opportunity. When they first met, he thought her eyes were simply plain brown but how he could see minute flecks of gold or green, changing according to her mood and the brightness of the light. The variety of the interchange of color fascinated him, and as corny as it felt, he never tired of looking into her eyes.

Randy looked away. He wasn't supposed to be studying her eyes. "I'm not exactly perfect, either. So if you'll overlook my flaws, I'll overlook yours, although I'm sure that you don't have many."

Her blush deepened, and she stared down at the table.

"I'm serious, Lacey. We're just going to be in the hot tub to get the stiffness out. Maybe we'll swim a few laps in the pool. It's right next to the hot tub." His words stalled. "Uh...you can swim, can't you?"

"Of course I can swim. I'm a little out of shape, but I actually swim very well."

"Then do you wanna race?"

"Pardon me?"

"I hope you don't take this the wrong way, but I have a feeling that neither of us get enough exercise during the week. Once a week, we should go swimming. You know, get some exercise. After all, it's free. It's not a big pool, but it's big enough."

"I don't know.... That may not be a good idea."

"Don't worry about it. I'll pick you up Saturday on my way home from my meeting. We can do brunch and then go for a swim, have a lounge in the hot tub, grab something for supper and then go to Eric and Susan's for the evening."

Lacey stared blankly at him. "Suddenly it feels like you've planned the whole day."

Randy grinned. "What if I have?" Quite frankly, he couldn't think of a better way to spend Saturday.

Lacey sighed. "Part of me wants to turn you down, but the smarter part of me says that what you're suggesting sounds perfect. I really do need to do something to get in shape, or at least do something so I won't get in worse shape."

Personally, Randy thought her shape was quite fine, but he bit his tongue until he flushed the testosterone from his brain. "Then we should think about getting together to swim every Saturday, after my meeting." He paused to check his watch. "I know it's only been fifteen minutes, but things are busy and we should probably get back out there."

Lacey stood. "This was a great idea, not just sitting, but getting away from the crowds. We'll have to do this more often."

Randy glanced around the storage room. One bare light bulb hung on a cord from the ceiling, which had water marks on it from a few years ago when the roof leaked during a rainstorm. Shelves piled with boxes lined two walls, a worktable strewn with computer parts and components and some of his tools and a bright lamp for precision work was pushed against the third wall. The small table, two chairs and a pile of the staff's personal belongings, including his inline skates, were against the fourth wall, where the door was.

The room was small, crowded, messy and dingy.

If Lacey was impressed with him taking her here, then he was losing his touch.

He stood. "Then for Saturday, it's a da…" He let his voice trail off. He'd almost said "date," although he didn't know where the thought came from. He wasn't going to play the dating game, now or anytime in the near future. Maybe never. And certainly not with Lacey.

He cleared his throat. "...Deal."

"Wow," Randy winced as he sank slowly into the padded restaurant chair. "Did anyone get the license number of that truck? I feel like I've been hit, and then run over a few times for good measure."

Lacey empathized as Randy massaged his upper arm at the same time as he flexed his elbow. "I know what you mean," she said as she also flexed the stiffness out of her own arms, at least temporarily. She knew she would be stiffer tomorrow. "I haven't had a workout like that for years, and it sure felt good to swim today."

Randy arched his back, then twisted from side to side as the waiter appeared beside their table. "I don't think I'm going to comment."

The waiter gave them both menus, filled their coffee cups, then left them alone to decide on their orders.

While Randy scanned the menu, Lacey scanned the restaurant. She'd been expecting a regular pizzeria, but Randy's friend's brother's restaurant was the farthest thing from a pizzeria she'd ever seen. Pizza wasn't even listed on the menu. Instead, many of the items were things she'd never heard of before. There was a large selection of pasta, beneath which the menu stated it was "proudly made on the premises by the Delanio family."

Without moving her head, Lacey tried to take in everything she could about the restaurant, which was as classic Italian as Italian could be. The decorating was set in rich earth tones, mostly browns and greens. The tablecloths were deep red and every table had a soft candle burning in the middle. Framed photographs of people and scenery lined the walls, and the rest of the decorating consisted of small sundry items that were probably native to different areas in Italy. The lights were dimmed, and soft romantic music played in the background. Even though there were many different-sized groups, ranging from two to eight or more people per table, there were no children. The youngest people she could see were a couple of teenagers who looked to be about sixteen, out on what could have been a first date.

And thinking of dates, Lacey leaned forward on the table and lowered her voice almost to a whisper as she spoke to Randy. "This isn't exactly what I had in mind, and I wouldn't call this a 'family' restaurant."

Randy massaged his upper arm, wincing as he pressed into the muscle with his fingertips. "But it is. It's owned by the Delanio family. And if you want to get technical, you're not exactly the definition of someone who swims 'well.'"

Lacey straightened and gently sipped her coffee,

closing her eyes for a few seconds to savor the rich blend. "I don't know what you mean."

"Don't give me that nonsense. I knew I was in trouble when the first thing you did was go straight to the diving board and do a double flip with that spinny move. You barely made a splash with your entry. I've seen it on television, but I've never actually known anyone who could do that."

Lacey knew *she* was in trouble the second they had entered the restaurant and been escorted to a cozy and private table for two that had a reserved sign on it. She also saw the owner, who would have been Randy's friend Tony, at the front counter, grinning when they walked in together.

"But I told you I could swim *very* well."

Randy snorted softly. "Up until today, I would have said that I swim very well, too. After all, I have a pool at my disposal all the time. I used to swim every day, but lately I've only had time to go once or twice a week. Still, when I asked you earlier if you wanted to race, I was just kidding. That *'very'* of yours was apparently a little understated, don't you think?"

"I don't know what you mean. You won twice."

He arched, and pressed his fists into the small of his back. "Yeah. Two out of seven, and I think you just let me win at least one of those two times before you graciously refused to do any more racing."

Lacey tried not to smile, and failed. "That's how I got my college scholarship. I was on my college swim team. We won the national championship that year. I don't like team sports, but racing is more a test of individual endurance. Today, when we started racing, I discovered I still have a bit of a competitive streak left in me."

"You didn't tell me that before."

Lacey set her coffee cup onto the saucer. "I could very easily remind you of something important that you didn't tell me and you probably should have."

She waited for an explanation, but instead, a silence hung in the air between them. As the silence continued, if it hadn't been for the soft music in the background to ease some of the tension, Lacey might have run away screaming.

When he finally spoke, Randy's voice came out in a husky whisper, and he stared down into his coffee cup, not looking at her. "The past is past. I wish it could be changed, but it can't."

Lacey's stomach rolled. "I know."

She wanted nothing more than to believe with all her heart that Randy would never, ever again pick up a drink and sink to the depths he once came from. But after watching Eric for years, she knew that it was difficult, sometimes impossible. She'd also seen some of Eric's drinking friends, and they were no different than Eric.

She couldn't understand the compulsion that kept a person drinking even though they knew it caused so much destruction to their own lives, as well as the lives of those around them. She wanted to understand the reason Randy had felt the need to let alcohol deaden his senses to the point where instead of controlling the alcohol he consumed, the alcohol controlled him. Except the thought terrified her that his reason for drinking might be something he'd done that would cause her to hate him.

Yet for the entire time she'd known Randy, he'd done nothing to cause her to doubt his faith, his sincerity, or his character.

She stared up into his face, into his beautiful eyes—eyes that shone with trustworthiness and something else she didn't want to acknowledge.

Randy sighed. "I don't want to get bogged down with past garbage, especially not tonight. But if you must, then ask me one question, just one. I'll answer honestly, no matter what, and then let's move on to something more pleasant."

Lacey didn't know what she would do if he told her that he drank because of the guilt from doing something terrible before he let the drinking get so bad it became an issue. Maybe she was in denial, but she couldn't believe Randy could have done anything so awful that it would cause a person to drink himself out of control. Therefore, she wondered if the reason he drank was because of something that someone had done to him.

It would almost make it acceptable if his reason for drinking was because he'd been a victim of something horrible, although she didn't want to think that he'd suffered. However, it would be best for her to know, as she knew people who could probably help him.

"Did someone do something to you that you're ashamed of?"

"No."

She waited for him to say more, but he didn't.

"Did you have an unhappy childhood?"

"That's two questions. Sorry."

Lacey gritted her teeth. Her next question would have been: Had someone broken his heart? Although, right now she wasn't sure she wanted to know the answer to that one.

Randy leaned forward on the table. "Do I get to ask you a question now? You asked me a question, and I answered."

She folded her hands in front of her and swallowed hard. "Fair is fair, I suppose. Go ahead."

Randy raised one hand and rested his index finger over the top of his upper lip. "Do you think I should grow a mustache?"

"What?" Lacey sputtered. She stared at his face. When they first met, she thought he was quite attractive, especially when he smiled. Not only did his dark blue eyes mesmerize her, the beginnings of laugh lines at the corners of those striking blue eyes made him more handsome than any man had a right to be. More than anything, those laugh lines were a visual indication of the most prominent parts of his personality—his optimistic outlook and his charming sense of humor. She didn't want him to change anything, including the way he looked.

"No. I don't think you should grow a mustache."

"Why not? Don't you think it would make me look more dignified?"

She didn't want him to grow a mustache because when the day came that he would kiss her again, she didn't want it to tickle.

Her breath caught as she realized the direction of her thoughts.

"That's two questions. Sorry."

Randy laughed just as the waiter arrived to take their orders.

Randy rested one finger on the menu. "I'll have the *Polla alla Parmigiana.*" He leaned forward to her and lowered his voice to a whisper. "This is my absolute favorite. Tony makes it even better than his mother."

Silence hung until Lacey realized that the waiter was waiting for her to give him her choices. Unfortunately, she'd been too busy checking out the decorating and not paying enough attention to the menu.

"I think I'll have this one." She pointed to the *Linguina Frutti di Mare,* recognizing the name from the supermarket, although she'd never tried it before.

"I'll be right back with some fresh bread for you."

The waiter picked up the menus and left.

"You could have taken more time if you weren't sure what you wanted."

"I know, but that one did sound good."

"It's all good. Whether Tony makes it or Mrs. Delanio."

While they waited for their meals to arrive, Randy filled her in with some tales from Bob's mother's kitchen. When the waiter finally delivered the food, Lacey's sides were beginning to hurt from so much laughing.

She wiped her eyes. "I think you should say grace. I'm not together enough."

Randy nodded. "Thanks, Lord, for this food, this time to get together and for the great day we've had so far. I pray for Your blessings on the rest of the evening—my time with Eric, and Lacey's time with Susan. Amen."

Lacey began to eat, immediately savoring the delicious meal. "Remember that we can't take too long here. What time does this evening's meeting start?"

"Seven o'clock. We'll be okay."

"Are things still going okay with Eric?"

"You know I'm not supposed to talk about that.

Anything you hear has to come from him. But I suppose I can say that he's doing about average, although I have mixed feelings about him leaving his own church and coming to mine while he gets his head together."

"Why?"

"Because he needs his nondrinking friends right now. I don't know if I could be where I am today if it wasn't for Bob, Adrian and Paul."

"Actually, I don't think he has any nondrinking friends left."

"That's too bad. No matter how stupid I was, Adrian, Bob and Paul were always there for me. I don't know what I would have done without them."

"It's great that God has blessed you with such good friends. Have you known them long?"

"We pretty much grew up together, and we do everything together, or at least we did until recently."

"Oh, dear. I hope you didn't have some kind of disagreement after all this time."

"It's not that. It's just that now Adrian's married and about to become a father, and Bob is about to get married. Paul is still single, like me, but he's been getting busier and busier with other stuff. I guess I have, too."

Lacey wondered if one thing Randy had been busy with was helping others the same way he was now helping Eric. If so, she considered that quite admirable.

They ate quickly, and Eric was ready and waiting when they arrived. As Eric and Randy left, Lacey walked into the living room to wait for Susan. When she sat on the couch, Kaitlyn climbed onto her lap.

"Auntie Lacey, will you tell me a story before bed?"

Lacey smiled. "Of course." Since she knew she was genetically predisposed to be a bad judge of male character, she wasn't likely to ever get married, which unfortunately meant she would never have children. But she loved both Shawn and Kaitlyn with all her heart, and they were the next best thing to a family of her own. "Go get a book you haven't seen for a while, and we can do that."

"I don't wants one of my books. I wants you to tell me a story with no book."

Lacey shuffled in her seat. "I don't know any stories without a book."

Kaitlyn threw her arms around Lacey's neck. "But I don't wants an old story. I wants a new one. I loves you, Auntie Lacey."

Lacey hugged her little niece back. "Okay, how's this then? Once upon a time, there were three little pigs."

"Auntie Lacey, that's not a new story."

Lacey pressed one finger to her lips, and Kaitlyn quieted. "Who were friends with a giant who was big and green and loved vegetables."

"Oh!"

"So the pigs introduced the giant to a princess. But some of his peas got under her mattress, and she couldn't sleep. So then—"

"I know! I know! The giant had a friend who was a frog, and the princess kissed the frog and he turned into a handsome prince. And then she married the prince!"

"Well, that's not exactly the way I would have ended the story, but I guess that works." She couldn't believe she'd put together such a mismatched story. It wasn't in her nature to do so such things. But it was something she could see Randy doing. She didn't want to think that Randy's convoluted ways were rubbing off on her.

Lacey patted her niece's head. "Come on, now. It's time to go to sleep."

She carried Kaitlyn to bed while Susan helped Shawn pick up some of his trucks that were in the living room, before putting him to bed.

"Let's say prayers."

"Auntie Lacey, has you ever kissed a frog?"

Gently Lacey pulled the blanket up and tucked it under Kaitlyn's chin. "No, sweetie, I've never kissed a frog." The last thing—or person—she had kissed was Randy. His kiss had been so gentle and sweet, and far too short.

She quickly pushed the thought from her mind. She shouldn't have been thinking about kissing Randy.

For a fleeting second, thinking about the princess kissing the frog who turned into a prince made her want to believe that such things could happen, that by kissing Randy, it would somehow have made him different.

But such things only happened in romance novels and fairy tales. Randy wasn't a perfect prince—he had been an alcoholic, with all the troubles and problems and risks that went with such an unstable background.

Lacey had seen too much of that in a man already in the lives of her mother and her sister, none of it good.

"Enough talk about kissing frogs. It's time to say your prayers."

Kaitlyn said a short but heartfelt prayer thanking God for her family, even her brother, and expressed her wishes that soon she would get a puppy. Once Kaitlyn was asleep, Lacey tiptoed out of the room to go sit on the couch.

Finally, Susan returned to the living room. "Sorry I took so long. Shawn didn't want to go to sleep until Randy got back. He's really taken a liking to Randy."

Lacey forced herself to smile. "I know. That kind of thing happens all the time."

Susan sighed. "I can see that. Everyone likes him. It would be easy for a woman to get stars in her eyes over him. I can't remember it ever being that way with Eric before we got married."

Lacey could certainly understand. Even back then, Lacey had seen Eric's potential problems, and he'd certainly lived up, or rather, down, to that expectation. Lacey hadn't liked Eric then, and she liked him even less now.

"No," Lacey said, "but you've got to remember that Randy is different from Eric."

Suddenly, something Randy said the day she found out about his history of alcoholism roared through her head, cutting off everything else she was going to say.

"You've got to remember that I'm different from Eric," he'd said.

She just said the same thing to Susan.

It was bad enough she was starting to tell stories Randy-style. She didn't want to start quoting him, too.

Lacey rose quickly from the couch and walked toward the kitchen. "How about if we make ourselves some tea before the guys get back?"

"Okay."

Susan didn't say anything while they flitted about in the kitchen, which Lacey found frustrating. Since Randy hadn't told her anything worthwhile about Eric's progress, or lack of progress—she didn't know which—she'd expected her sister to at least say something.

But Susan said nothing about it, almost like she was avoiding the topic. They talked about everything else, even the weather.

The weather didn't interest Lacey unless it was going to rain on Monday morning, because she didn't want to think of Randy getting wet while skating to work.

Lacey dragged one hand down her face.

Randy. Again he was invading her brain.

"Lacey, do you think we should make some cookies? They might want a snack when they come back."

"We don't have time to make cookies. They should be back in twenty minutes."

Susan smiled. "Then that's perfect. The dough is in the fridge. All I have to do is cut the pieces and put them in the oven. Randy won't take anything for helping Eric, so this is one small way I can show my appreciation."

"He'll like that. He loves sweets. He especially has a thing for Boston Creme doughnuts."

"I'll have to remember that, but for now, the cookies will have to do. Can you get out the cookie sheet?"

Something in Lacey's gut clenched. She didn't want to know what Randy's favorite treat was. And she had a feeling that he probably did make cookies for himself, because she already knew he was a good cook. She also suspected that if he ever made himself a special treat, he probably worked it off in the pool. He'd told her that he often went for a swim alone, after everyone else was in bed and the pool was supposed to be closed.

She wondered if she started hitting herself in the head with the cookie sheet, if this time she could exorcise thoughts of Randy.

While they waited for the cookies to bake, Lacey put on a pot of coffee, knowing Randy would want some, and she didn't want to think of why she knew that drinking coffee late in the evening didn't affect him.

The front door opened at the same time as the oven timer dinged. Both men appeared in the kitchen as Susan scooped the last cookie from the sheet onto a cooling tray.

Randy grinned from ear to ear as he focused on the hot cookies. "Did you miss me?"

Lacey had actually missed him much more than she wanted to, so she chose to say nothing.

Guilt poked at her for being less than charitable. Randy had done nothing to deserve her bad attitude. It was her own fault that she couldn't stop thinking about him, not his. As always, Randy had done nothing but remain helpful, cheerful and supportive.

Just looking at his handsome, smiling face, she felt compelled to somehow make it up to him, for all her negative thoughts.

"Why don't you guys go sit in the living room, and we'll be right out with everything?"

Eric did exactly as she said, and immediately went to sit on the couch.

Randy poured two cups of coffee and topped up her tea, added the milk to the coffee, tucked a pile of napkins under his arm and carried both mugs into the living room, carefully setting them on magazines when he couldn't find coasters.

Susan took her tea in one hand and the plate of cookies in the other, while Lacey carried her own tea and a small handful of spoons.

The only one empty-handed had been Eric.

"So, how was the meeting?" she asked, trying to act casual as she passed the plate to Randy once they were all seated.

"Good," he said, then reached for a cookie. "We got a parking spot right near the door."

She waited for him to continue, but he didn't.

"That's it? You got a good parking spot?"

"We got good seats close to the front, too."

"And?"

"And the speakers were really interesting. Next week they're going to have a ten-year cake. That's a biggie."

Again, she waited for him to continue. He didn't. Therefore, she turned to Eric, but she didn't know what to say, as she didn't think that asking him if he had a "nice time" was quite the right thing to say. She didn't want to be so blunt as to come right out and ask if he learned anything, but she wanted to know so badly it was nearly painful.

She stared at Eric very pointedly, until he began to squirm. "I guess you're expecting me to say something. I'm not really sure what to think yet, except that there are a lot more people involved than I thought there would be. While I've seen a few of the same people at both meetings, most of the people at each place are different. I didn't know there would be so many." He turned to Randy.

Randy shrugged his shoulders. "I think the total numbers would surprise you. But as to attendance, everybody's different. Most people go to a meeting almost every day for the first year. Some people go to three or four meetings a week for the rest of their lives. Some go to one meeting a week, sometimes less. And then there's everything in between. I've been sober for just over six years, and I only go to one meeting a week, unless I'm taking someone else. You have to do what's best for you. I can't make that decision. All I can do is go with you and be there for you, for as long as you need me."

Instead of waiting for Eric to respond, Randy gulped the last of his coffee down in one gulp and stood. "Come on, Lacey. I think it's time to go."

"Go? But…" She let her voice trail off. As they had the last time, they'd come in separate cars, so there really was no need for both of them to leave at the same time.

Unless Randy knew something she didn't.

She stood, as well. "Of course. What was I thinking?"

The second the door closed behind them, he turned to her. "We have to talk. Follow me to the doughnut shop."

He strode to his car without giving her any chance for rebuttal.

Dutifully she followed him. He didn't say a word to her until they were sitting down.

"Just in case you're wondering, I didn't want to get too comfy at their place because I wanted something that one of the speakers said to sink in a little more, and that wasn't going to happen with us there."

"I don't understand."

"I know you've never been to an AA meeting, but what happens for most of the meeting is that different people go up to the front and say whatever is on their minds. The last guy had a lot to say about his wife and his marriage, about how happy he is being together. He's been married, to the same woman, for twenty-three years and they've had a lot of ups and downs, but he loves her to the bottom of his heart and soul. Some of the stuff he said was even making some of the guys sniffle." One corner of his mouth tilted up. "Although now that it's over, no one will admit it." His expression again turned serious. "Anyway, I thought it best to leave Eric alone with Susan so he sees that things could turn out the same for him. If he works at it, that is."

Lacey was almost surprised at his words, but then, his involvement with Eric began when he'd witnessed Susan crying over the state of her marriage. "That's such a sweet sentiment. No wonder women fall all over you."

He shrugged his shoulders. "Nah. Mostly I just like to hear myself talk. That's why I'm good in retail sales. Sometimes I think I'd make a good deejay on the radio, except they have to start out on the night shift, and then I'd be all alone for a whole eight hours in a row, every single night, and I think that would drive me nuts."

Lacey opened her mouth, about to say that he would make a good deejay. He was easy to listen to, he did like to talk, and also, he was great with the sound system at church, so she knew that kind of thing would be easy for him.

Instead, she snapped her mouth shut. Again, he'd changed the subject, and she'd almost fallen for it.

"Quit that. That's not what I was talking about, and you know it. I saw a few of the ladies in your church watching you." More than that, Lacey felt them watching *her*, because she was with Randy.

"I don't know why. I really don't date much. In fact, I don't even remember the last time I had a steady girlfriend."

She didn't know if she wanted to hear about his

experiences with other women, but Randy was an enigma, and she wanted to learn more about him. "Why not?"

"I just don't." He looked down at her plate, and seeing that she had finished her muffin, Randy rammed the last of his doughnut into his mouth, and stood. "I have to get up early for church in the morning. I think it's time to go."

"Go? But…" Even though she knew he had to be at church an hour early, Lacey doubted the time was really the issue. She had the feeling that again she was pushing her toes past another dotted line with Randy, a line he didn't want her to cross. The more she got to know him, the more she discovered she didn't know. Except for a few small smatterings of information, she didn't know anything about him prior to the day he'd quit drinking, which made her want to know more about the "real" Randy, the one he kept hidden. She could understand that he might have done things when he was drinking that he wanted to forget about, and he could do that. Randy was a new creation in God's sight, and he could close that door. But at the same time, she wanted to know what motivated him to do what he did, which she couldn't know until she learned more of the "old" Randy.

But that wasn't going to happen tonight. He was already standing, and waiting for her to do the same.

So Lacey followed his lead and stood, too. "You're right. It is getting late. Let's go."

They exited the building and walked side by side through the parking lot, until they reached their cars, which were parked together.

He escorted her to the driver's door of her car and waited while she unlocked it.

"I guess I'll see you at church," she said as she pulled the door open. Lacey turned around, intending to wish him good-night, but her words caught in her throat.

The night was dark, but the glow of the lights from above shone on Randy like a spotlight, highlighting his dark hair and emphasizing his broad shoulders, and most of all, it intensified the shimmer in Randy's striking blue eyes, eyes that could probably make women faint at his feet. She saw it all the time. Every woman who came in contact with him liked him.

"Good night, Lacey," he murmured as he shuffled closer.

Lacey's heart increased in tempo as they stood nearly toe to toe. Very slowly he raised one hand, then stopped with it hovering in midair, just below her chin.

Lacey's eyes drifted shut all by themselves. She tipped her chin up and parted her lips slightly, waiting, meeting him halfway.

Very gently and tenderly his fingertips brushed her cheek, then slid behind her ear. Slowly the warmth of his thumb rubbed her temple.

Her lower lip started to quiver, and she couldn't stop it. She squeezed her eyes shut even harder.

His voice came out in a husky whisper. "I guess I'll see you in church." The warmth of his hand suddenly disappeared. She counted four footsteps in quick succession before her eyes opened. By that time he'd clicked the electronic lock of his car, and he was inside before she had time to blink. The second the motor started, he was gone.

She moved quickly into her car, shutting the door as his car turned out of the parking lot.

"Good night, Randy," she whispered to the empty street.

Chapter Seven

Randy grumbled to himself as he set the last control to get the sound he wanted. He was having a particularly hard time getting everything right, but he also knew the reason.

He was allowing himself to become distracted. Every time someone new walked into the sanctuary, he kept looking up to see if it was Lacey.

And every time it wasn't.

The service was ready to start, and she still wasn't there.

He had a bad feeling he knew why. He'd almost lost it last night. He'd wanted to kiss her again, but at the last minute, he'd bolted.

He couldn't kiss her, because he didn't have that right.

But she would have kissed him. Any fool could have seen that.

And he was a fool.

In the privacy of the sound room booth, Randy closed his eyes and pressed his hands over his face. *Lord God, don't let her hate me. Tell me what to do.*

Behind him, the door creaked open. He quickly lowered his hands and tapped one of the control knobs.

"Hi, Randy. Sorry I'm late. Kaitlyn wouldn't leave without her favorite teddy bear, and we almost couldn't find it."

He turned around to smile, his heart pounding so hard he was positive Lacey could hear it. "No problem. I was just beginning to wonder if you were going to make it."

She sighed. "I hate walking into church after everything has started, although I do know a lot of people at my church who arrive promptly five minutes after the service begins, week after week."

"Yeah. Same here."

The music of the first song ended. Randy set the PowerPoint to a scenery picture as Paul stepped closer to the microphone and welcomed everyone. Randy adjusted the volume levels while the congregation greeted one another at Paul's invitation.

He watched Lacey out of the corner of his eye as she stood at the window. When his friends on the worship team waved at the window, Lacey waved back.

"I know you can't tell me what was said at the meeting, but whatever it was, you were right. Eric's been different this morning. He didn't lose his temper when Kaitlyn couldn't find her bear. He even helped find it instead of storming off and waiting in the car while Susan did everything."

"Good. Just remember, though, that this isn't going to be an instant, overnight change. There will be ups and there will be downs."

"I know. But I thought you'd like to know that we've started to see some ups."

At Lacey's words, last night's speaker's words echoed through his head like a clanging gong. The man had been emphatic in telling everyone at the meeting, both men and the women, to respect and nurture that special someone God put into their paths, because often, there were no second chances. And if there was a second chance, to grab it and never let it go.

Up until last night, Randy hadn't considered that with his history, he was capable of being involved in a nurturing relationship; he couldn't participate because he thought he had nothing to give. But last night in the parking lot, it had hit him that he could be wrong.

Lacey would have kissed him. She wouldn't have been open to him if she didn't see something in him, even if he didn't know what he possibly had to offer.

Yet at the same time, Randy tried his best to live his life the way God wanted him to. He treated people the way he would have wanted to be treated if the situation were reversed. He was a good friend to the men in his life, but he hadn't thought he had it in him to be a good friend to the women, as well. He especially hadn't thought he was capable of treating Lacey the way she deserved to be treated in God's sight.

But there was something happening here, between himself and Lacey, no matter how hard he tried to fight it. And it was breaking him down.

In the parking lot at the bar, he knew he'd caught her off guard when he leaned over the seat and kissed her. In fact, he'd caught himself off guard, but he did it anyway.

The kiss had been different…special. He'd always rolled his eyes when Carol talked about her fiancé's kiss being like fireworks, but he couldn't think of any better way to describe how it felt when he'd kissed Lacey that night.

Randy squeezed his eyes shut. The first time he'd kissed Lacey had been in the parking lot at a bar, the second time, when he could have kissed her, was at the doughnut shop. Was he such a loser that he could only kiss a woman in a parking lot? Why was everything he did that was worth anything, ultimately self-destructive?

"Randy? Are you okay? Do you need to lie down or something?"

His eyes shot open. For now he was fine, but he didn't want to stress himself into what he knew could happen. He didn't ever want Lacey to see him like that. "Don't worry. I'm fine. I was just thinking about something. Excuse me. It looks like Paul's ready to start."

He quickly set the PowerPoint to the next song, and because it was the first song, he concentrated on getting the sound level settings right as it progressed.

About halfway through the song, Lacey leaned toward him. "It feels so strange not singing on Sunday morning. Last time we were together in here was different, being the first time, but today it really feels like something's missing."

"I know what you mean. For now I'm making adjustments, but when I'm alone and I've got everything right, I sit in here and sing all by myself. So go ahead and sing, too. No one can hear us because there's a lot more sound out there than in here. I promise. In a way, it's perfect up here, because only God hears me if I sing off-key. So please, don't be shy."

"It's okay. I'll just listen."

"Don't worry. It took me a while to get used to this. It's almost like singing in the shower, except here, there's actual music to sing to, the sound system is really good, and there's no echo."

When Lacey turned to stare at him, he felt his face heat up as he thought of what he'd just admitted.

"Don't look at me like that. I know I'm not the

only human being on this earth who sings in the shower. I just admit it."

"That might be a little more information than I need to know."

The burn of his blush extended to his ears. "Sorry. I was just making a point, and I think I got carried away. Anyway, it's okay to sing up here."

Sometimes when his friends were doing their pre-service practicing not only did Randy sing all by himself up in the sound room, but sometimes when his friends were going over the same part over and over to get it right, Randy pretended he was singing into a microphone to help the time pass.

But when the service was in session and everyone sang to worship God, Randy settled down, singing just as if he were sitting in the sanctuary with the rest of the congregation.

He flicked the PowerPoint to the next screen, turned to Lacey and grasped her hands. "Please don't be shy. I don't want to hamper your worship this morning, or any Sunday morning."

Paul led the congregation right into singing the next song, so Randy followed along and began to sing, just like everyone else. The only difference between this and any other Sunday was that with Lacey so close to him, he sang much more softly than he usually did.

After a few lines, Lacey began to sing with him.

The experience was like nothing he'd ever experienced. Lacey sang exactly on pitch, her voice blending perfectly with his. So perfect, that Randy stopped singing the melody and began to sing in harmony. They were beautiful together.

They sang all the songs that way. At times, Randy could barely get his voice to work, for the wonder of the experience, but at the same time it felt so right that he couldn't not sing.

The last song was about trusting in God, and asking for God's guidance in times of uncertainty.

When all voices had quieted, the music continued to play, lower in volume, which Randy knew meant Paul was giving the congregation more time so everyone could continue to soak in the words and the impact of the song. Today, Randy also needed more time to let everything sink in. He couldn't remember the last time he'd been so affected by the music during the service.

He faded the words on the screen instead of abruptly making them disappear, then turned to Lacey.

He froze, staring into her deep brown eyes.

They were beautiful eyes, full of sincerity, reverence of God Almighty and something else he was afraid to define.

With all voices silent, with God's music playing softly in the background, something passed between them, but he didn't know what.

A peace he'd never known settled over him.

This moment was another turning point of his life. If only he could figure out what it was.

"I'm so glad you could come."

"I'm glad we did. This was really, great, right, Eric?"

Lacey stepped back and watched as Randy moved closer to Eric, waiting for Eric's response.

"Yeah. Your church is really different than ours."

Randy smiled politely. "I don't think that's necessarily true. I think you were just seeing things differently. Today, maybe for the first time, you were ready to let God touch you."

Lacey noticed that Eric didn't comment. But she had a feeling that Randy's words were accurate. Only Eric didn't want to admit it.

Randy glanced back and forth between Eric and Susan. "How would you all like to go out for lunch—my treat?"

Susan's mouth dropped open. "No, I can't let you do that. That's too much. Besides, I already have a lunch prepared at home. Why don't you come to our house? We'd love to have you." Susan turned to Lacey. "Of course, you're invited, too, especially since your car is still at our house."

"Uh. Sure." Randy glanced over his shoulder. "Just let me tell the guys. Eric, how would you like to come with me? You were saying you might be interested in playing guitar. I can introduce you to Adrian. He hasn't been playing all that long, but he's really quite good. He could probably give you some tips."

Eric nodded and began to walk away with Randy. Since they hadn't picked up the children from their Sunday school classrooms yet, that left Lacey alone with Susan.

The second the men were out of earshot, Lacey spoke. "What do you think?"

Susan turned her head as Randy and Eric disappeared around the corner, then reappeared atop the stage platform. "I think he's perfect. He's crazy about you."

Lacey felt a burn in her cheeks. "I meant, what did you think about Eric during the service?" Lacey pointed up to the sound booth's window at the rear of the sanctuary. During the service Randy had warned her not to be distracted by watching people, but she couldn't help it. "I had an unfair advantage. Every once in while, I looked at Eric from up there. It's really quite a different perspective from so high. I could see what everybody did for the whole length of the service. Eric seemed to be really paying attention."

"What were you doing up there?"

"Last week they had a guest speaker, but this week Randy couldn't leave the booth because he had to do the PowerPoint for the pastor's sermon, so I stayed up there with him. I could see everything from up there."

Susan shrugged her shoulders. "I thought Eric was paying attention to the pastor, but I don't know what he was thinking. I'll have to see later this evening if he wants to talk about it."

"So far so good, then."

Susan turned again to the stage, where Eric was shaking hands with Adrian. "Last night I didn't want to ask in case the kids were listening, but today it's killing me. I have to know. How was your date last night?"

Lacey gritted her teeth. "It wasn't a date."

"No, you're right. A date would have been just dinner. You spent all day with Randy, too. What did you do?"

"We went swimming for the afternoon. Then we went out for dinner."

Susan's eyes widened. "Swimming? And you're still together? I'm even more impressed. Not only is he smart and funny, that means he's a gracious loser, too."

"That's beside the point. Things between me and Randy aren't exactly what you're thinking. He's still an alcoholic, and I don't know what to do with him. We've both seen the same thing so many times with both Dad and Eric. Things go well for a while, but then something happens and everything goes right back to the way it was. I can't live like that."

As soon as the words came out of her big mouth, Lacey immediately wished she could take them back.

She'd had those same thoughts for years, but never voiced them, especially not to Susan.

Susan's smile dropped, and her voice came out in a hoarse whisper. "I know. But this time, things are different. Eric has Randy to help him. You have to understand that Eric doesn't have any friends who quit drinking, because if they quit, they wouldn't be friends anymore. I'm sure there are lots of people out there who quit and don't go back. It's just that I don't know any of them. Except for Randy."

Lacey wished that Susan would quit holding Randy up as a shining example of perfection at every opportunity. While six years was a long time at the present moment, especially compared to Eric's longest period of sobriety, which was thirty-nine days, the space of six years was dust in the wind compared to a lifetime.

"Hi. Did you miss me?"

Lacey spun around to see Randy, with Eric at his side, stopping to stand behind her.

Fortunately, Eric picked up Susan's hand and started to speak before she had to reply to Randy. "Randy's friend said that he'd show me a few things on the guitar so I could see if it was something I wanted to do. All I have to do is buy a starter guitar."

Randy stepped closer. "I suggested that Eric put the money he would have spent at the bar into a special jar, and use that for the guitar. Then if he decides he likes it, he can keep saving in the jar and using that money for lessons. Then it wouldn't really be an extra expense. That's what I did when I first quit drinking. It didn't take too long, and I'd saved up enough money to get my first digital camera." He broke out into a wide grin, and his eyes sparkled with joy. "I've kept putting money in the jar, and I've bought some really neat things. My digital camera, of course, and the greatest DVD player. And you should see my new MP3 player. Right now I'm saving for a wide-screen television." Randy's smile widened, and he reached to the clip on his belt. "Let me show you the latest thing I got with my jar money. This new cell phone. It does text messaging, documents, e-mail and takes great high-resolution pictures."

Eric stared blankly at the phone. If Randy had made a reference to a new fishing rod and reel, then Eric's interest would have been piqued. Electronic gadgetry didn't impress Eric, probably because he was usually too drunk to understand how anything high-tech worked, and he refused to read directions when he was sober.

"Uh, that's nice," Eric said, "but what do you do when you just need to make a phone call?"

Lacey rested her hand on Randy's forearm. "I think maybe we should start getting ready to go. Do you have to help your friends pack up?"

Randy clipped the phone back onto his belt. "Not

this time. No one is using the building this afternoon, so we can go now."

As Lacey turned around, Eric and Susan disappeared to collect their children, telling her without words that they expected her to travel back to their house with Randy, not with them, even though they'd arrived together.

Once at the house, Lacey automatically joined Susan in the kitchen, where they finished the last details of preparing their lunch.

When Lacey walked into the living room to call everyone to the table, Eric was sitting on the couch watching television, but Randy was sitting cross-legged in the middle of the living room floor, surrounded by colored plastic bricks.

Randy held up a black plane, flicked the plastic propeller with his finger, then swooshed the plane through the air, making the sound of a jet engine as the plane zoomed along its path.

Shawn stood behind Randy holding a second plane very similar to Randy's. Shawn made a higher-pitched version of the same jet engine noise with his propeller-type plane, circled the room once, then dove headfirst under the end table.

Lacey crossed her arms. "What are you doing?"

Randy looked up at her from his place on the floor. "We're building stuff."

Lacey rested her fists on her hips. "Lunch is ready."

Randy landed his plane, complete with all the appropriate noises, then taxied the plane to a large multicolored brick structure with a box on top that had squares drawn on it, which was probably supposed to be the airport terminal, then stood. Shawn simply set his plane down on the floor where he was, and ran to Randy.

Adoration glowed in Shawn's eyes as he looked up. "Are we going to make more after lunch?"

Randy mussed Shawn's hair. "I don't know. Us grown-ups have some stuff to talk about. If we don't build the hangar today, we'll do it next time I come over. Let's eat first, then we'll see."

"Yay! Lunch! I bet it's pancakes!" Shawn squealed as he ran into the kitchen, with his sister hot on his heels. Eric leaned to the side, groping for the remote to turn off the television.

Lacey lowered her voice so only Randy could hear her. "What in the world are you doing playing with Shawn? Aren't you supposed to be talking with Eric?"

Randy lowered his voice and bent down toward her. "I couldn't with the kids in the room. Besides, did you see that bin of bricks? I kept mine from when I was a kid, but it's nothing like this."

"Aren't you a little old for that?"

Randy's eyebrows arched, as if he couldn't understand why she was asking.

Lacey rolled her eyes. "Come on."

She knew Eric and Susan didn't stop to say grace before every meal, but since it was Sunday, and since she was there, she knew they would today. The children politely bowed their heads and folded their hands on top of the table and waited.

Eric folded his hands, but instead of bowing his head, he turned toward his son. "Why don't you say the prayer today, Shawn?"

Shawn nodded. His words came out slowly and respectfully, and very solemn, as they did every Sunday when Lacey joined them for lunch. "Thanks, God, for this good lunch and for my family and for this beautiful day." He paused, then sucked in a deep breath. "And-thanks-for-my-new-airport-terminal-and-don't-let-my-sister-break-it-amen," he spewed out in rapid-fire succession.

Susan's head bobbed up. "Shawn!" she hissed.

Shawn didn't raise his head. "But I don't want Kaitlyn to wreck the new terminal I made with Randy."

Susan turned to Randy. "I'm so sorry. He's not usually like this."

Randy shrugged his shoulders. "It's okay. I'm actually kind of flattered that he thinks so much of our creation." He turned to Shawn. "But really, Shawn, it doesn't matter if anyone breaks it, including your sister. If someone breaks it, then you get to build it again, and building it is most of the fun. In fact, if it does get broken, then the next time you build it, it gets better."

"Really?"

Randy nodded. "Really. When I was your age, me and my friend Bob used to build stuff all the time, but sometimes his brothers Gene or Tony would need a special piece. Their mother made us share, so we had to take it apart. But it wasn't so bad. Lots of times the new one was better than the first time."

Lacey rested her hand on Randy's arm. "I saw Tony at the restaurant yesterday. It's good that you still remained friends with him, even though he destroyed your pet projects."

Randy grinned. "You bet. It didn't do any good to get mad at him, although sometimes we still did."

"You must have known your friend Bob for a long time, if you made childhood projects together."

"Yup."

Shawn tugged at Randy's shirt. "Do you still build airports with Bob?"

"No. We build grown-up things, now." Randy smiled. "I learned how to build computers, and Bob learned how to build cars. Or rather, he rebuilds them."

"Wow…" Shawn's voice trailed off.

Lacey studied Randy's face while Randy stared off into space, grinning at a memory he wasn't sharing.

Every time she'd seen Randy with Bob, as well as his friends Paul and Adrian, it was obvious that

they'd had many happy childhood memories together. Lacey didn't ever see any of her old childhood
friends, because she hadn't had many. They'd had to
move at a critical time because her mother couldn't
make the house payments, and after that their family tended to stick together because they'd had to
move into a much rougher neighborhood than they
had been used to. It had been at that time in their lives
when Susan had met Eric. Because Eric had been the
best pick of available men, Lacey had chosen to simply spend her time alone.

Randy leaned down. "So sharing is good, even
though it's not always fun at the time. I think it would
be nice of you to take Kaitlyn after lunch and show
her how to build something."

"I don't wanna make stuff with Shawn," Kaitlyn
whined. "I wanna play with my puppies."

Lacey turned to Randy. "She doesn't mean real
puppies. She has a family of toy dogs that she's quite
attached to."

Susan smiled weakly. "We can't have a real dog
right now. We might get one in a few years, after
Kaitlyn is in grade two."

Randy lost his smile. "I know what you mean, but
if I can stick my nose in where it doesn't belong,
please don't promise them a dog, and then not get one
when you said you would. My parents told me the
same thing. Except that when I finally did get old

enough, they came up with another reason. The reasons kept changing until I just gave up. I just wish they would have told me no, if they had no intention of keeping their promise. Of course I certainly understand why you don't want a dog now, and I certainly agree. I'm just saying, don't get their hopes up if you can't deliver."

Eric nodded. "Don't worry. We mean it. One day we'll have a dog. Just not yet."

They left the dishes, and Susan stayed in the kitchen to make coffee while everyone else moved to the living room to talk.

Lacey wished the conversation would have moved to something that could help Eric, but with the children playing at their feet, then Randy moving down to the floor to build more onto their ever-expanding airport complex, conversation topics were limited to what was acceptable for the children to hear. It didn't take long before Kaitlyn settled into Randy's lap, asking for help, which he gladly gave.

After the fleet had been expanded to include two more planes, Randy lifted Kaitlyn off his lap and set her onto the floor beside him.

"I hate to cut the afternoon short, but I have to start thinking about having an early supper. I have to be back at the church early to get ready for the evening service."

Lacey stood, as well. "You're right. We should go."

At her "we" reference, Randy hesitated. Now that they were back at Eric and Susan's house, she had her own car, so she could have stayed if she wanted to. It was just that she really didn't want to.

Susan and Eric escorted them to the door together. Randy very politely thanked Susan for the lunch, reminded Eric of their scheduled meeting for the next evening, then followed Lacey to her car instead of going to his own.

"I have an idea. Instead of going out to a restaurant, how would you like to do something else?"

"I guess. What do you have in mind?"

"I want to take you to the lagoon at the park."

"The lagoon? Whatever for?"

"Summer is almost over, and I want to take advantage of the last of the good weather. They have great hot dogs at the concession, and I would really like to walk around the lagoon and feed the ducks."

"I don't think ducks eat hot dogs."

He smiled.

Something in Lacey's stomach went haywire, making her think that maybe she was starting to get hungry again.

"The hot dogs will be for us. I was going to stop off at a convenience store and buy bread for the ducks. I figure we can make it once around and still have plenty of time to get to church for the evening service."

Lacey turned toward the street, although she didn't know why, because she couldn't see the park from where they were.

Randy was right. The children had all gone back to school, and already the temperatures were cooler. The leaves had already begun to change color. As far as she knew, the swans were gone, but the last of the ducks had not yet begun their migration south for the winter. Today was sunny and still warm, but even for tomorrow, the forecast was calling for cooler temperatures and rain.

Lacey inserted the key into the lock. "That sounds like a great idea. But what are we going to do about my car? It doesn't make sense to take both cars, but I don't want to leave it here."

"We can go the long way and drop it off at the church, and take my car from there. If that's okay with you." He lowered his voice. "Assuming that you want to come to the evening service with me."

"Of course I do. Let's go."

When they arrived at the park, true to his word, the first thing they did was buy hot dogs, and they immediately set out toward the lagoon.

Because it was Randy's idea to feed the ducks, he carried the loaf of bread in one hand while he ate his hot dog with the other.

Once they reached the circular path around the lagoon, they slowed their pace.

"Here. Go feed this to those ducks over there, and I'll take your picture."

Lacey's feet froze on the spot. "Picture? What are you talking about?"

He pulled his cell phone off his belt. "I never go anywhere without my phone."

In the back of her mind, she recalled Randy's skewed reference to the cell phone's abilities to take pictures when he was talking about his various gadgets to Eric.

"I don't like having my picture taken."

"Why not? This isn't for a fashion magazine. It's a permanent record of a fun day. I hope we're going to have fun, anyway."

"Okay, but only if you make sure you take the pictures of the ducks, not of me. I'll just throw the pieces and let them walk up to me as close as they dare, and you can take pictures of them at my feet."

"I can live with that."

As she said, Lacey crumbled up a slice of bread, dropped the pieces on the ground, then backed up so the ducks would come onto the shore and Randy could take their picture.

Lacey turned to look up at Randy just as a particularly large duck came within a few feet to check out what she'd dropped. Instead of taking the picture of the duck, the phone looked suspiciously like it was aimed at her, while she just happened to have her mouth open, and not at the duck who was on the ground at her feet.

"Hey! You said you weren't going to take any pictures of me."

"Sorry. I couldn't help myself. But don't worry, it's not a big deal. It's just for fun. No one will see it except me."

Immediately, she felt churlish. "I'm sorry. I guess I'm just not used to having my picture taken." More than that, no one had ever wanted to take her picture, except at Shawn and Kaitlyn's birthday parties, and then, most of the pictures were of the children, which was as it was supposed to be.

He lowered the phone, aimed it at the duck and pressed a button. "There. I got one of the duck, if that makes you happy. Want to see?" He pushed a few more buttons and turned the phone so she could see the picture that displayed in the small screen. First he showed her the picture of the duck, then the picture was of her, which actually did have the duck in it, except it was just the duck's head.

She couldn't help but smile. It wasn't a great picture, but it was good enough to recall the day together, which was the point of taking pictures in the first place.

After the duck ate the bread, they continued on their way. They hadn't gone far when Randy's hand slipped over her own, and his fingers intertwined with hers.

Part of her wanted to pull away, but part of her was actually enjoying his gentle touch, especially when they passed other couples who were also holding hands while they walked.

"Lacey, I was wondering—"

Suddenly Lacey stopped, pulling Randy to a halt, as well. She pointed to the water, where a bright-colored mallard and his brown-colored mate floated serenely in the water side by side. "Look! Aren't they beautiful?"

Randy smiled hesitantly. "Yeah, I guess so." They both turned, still hand in hand, and facing the lagoon, watched the ducks together.

"You know," Randy said, "I should get a picture of this. I don't know if I've ever seen a mated pair like that together, just the two of them, and been so close. In a way, it's kind of romantic."

"R-romantic?" Lacey stammered. "They're ducks…."

"I know geese mate for life. I think swans do, too. I'm not sure about ducks. I think some do. I'll have to look it up on the Internet when I get home tonight." Randy pulled his hand away, and immediately Lacey felt the loss. Randy unclipped his phone from his belt and walked to the water's edge. Lacey followed him.

He turned his head and grinned at her. "Watch. This is how it's done." He showed her the sequence of buttons to push to take the picture, then handed the phone to her.

Following his instructions, she took the first picture she'd taken in more years than she could remember.

She couldn't help but smile. "Maybe it's time I bought a camera. But I mean a real camera, not a phone disguised as a camera."

Randy smiled as he studied the small screen. "For a phone, it still takes fairly good pictures. I just got a great idea." He pulled a slice of bread out of the bag, laid the bag on the ground and stepped beside her. "I'm going to feed them. Press this button right here when they take it out of my hand. This model does a streaming video, but it only goes for fifteen seconds, so don't start too soon. Or you can just press it real fast when you want to take a picture. Then it will take only a couple of frames at a time, and I can use those for single photos."

Lacey stepped back and positioned the phone so she could watch Randy and the ducks on the view-screen at the same time, but the ducks didn't move closer. Instead, they only started to float away. "I can get you and the ducks in the same picture, but from here, they're only little dots."

Randy stepped forward until the tips of his shoes were nearly in the water. He leaned forward and extended his arm as far as he could, holding out the piece of bread. "Maybe they'll come back," he muttered.

Lacey stepped back and took one picture that included both Randy and the ducks. "It's okay. I'm sure you'll remember that those dots are the ducks."

Randy straightened. "Wait. I'm going to try something. I need to get closer." Cautiously Randy stepped onto one of the large rocks protruding from the water.

"What are you doing?!" Lacey gasped.

He stepped onto the next rock, then slowly, balancing on his toes, turned to face her. "I said, I'm going in closer. They're starting to move away. If this works, it will be great. There's a demo printer at the store that prints photo-quality pictures. For a while I thought about buying one, but that would tempt me to print every picture I took, so I've been storing all my photos on CD's. With a picture like this, especially out of the phone, which isn't as good as my digital camera, I can see how good the printer works because this will be a real shot, not something doctored up from the demo package."

Lacey shook her head. In a skewed way, she not only followed what he'd just said, she agreed with his logic. It was a scary concept.

He stepped out farther and farther onto the rock, then turned around, looking down as the ducks swam closer to him, probably wondering what a human was doing in the middle of their pond. Slowly Randy bent down until he was squatting. He tore a piece off the slice of bread and held it out.

Lacey shuddered. "Aren't you afraid they're going to bite you?" she called out from her safe position on the shoreline. "They may be used to people, but they're still wild animals."

"They're just ducks, not mountain lions. Shh. Here they come."

Time dragged in slow motion as the ducks slowly approached Randy as he remained motionless on the rock, the piece of bread extended at arm's length.

Lacey felt she should start taking pictures, but she wanted to get the best one, which would be of a duck actually taking the bread from Randy's hand.

"You should see what this looks like," she said softly as she concentrated on the viewfinder. "It looks like you're standing on the water."

"It almost feels like I am," he said softly, but not softly enough. The ducks stopped their approach. Just in case they didn't come any closer, Lacey pushed the button for her second picture of the day.

"Here, ducky ducky," Randy whispered melodically, reaching farther over the water with the piece of bread. "I have a yummy snack for you."

Lacey pressed the button, meaning to take a few frames, but suddenly the male duck spread its wings, causing the female duck to do the same. With the unexpected movement, Randy jerked back.

Lacey's finger froze on the button as the ducks flapped their wings, beginning the sequence to take flight. At the same time, Randy flailed his arms, but he wasn't getting ready to fly—he was attempting to regain his balance.

The piece of bread flew up into the air as Randy continued to fail his arms. He started to straighten, then extended one leg to hop back onto the larger rock in an attempt to get more solid footing. He jumped, but with all his movement, instead of landing firm, his shoe slid forward and he toppled backward.

The ducks rose above the surface of the water just as the splash resounded below.

Chapter Eight

Randy sputtered as he rose out of the cold water. His clothes stuck to his skin, his hair was plastered down over his head and water streamed down his face, causing him to shudder.

"Randy! Randy!" Lacey screamed from the safe, dry shoreline, her arms waving in the air. "Are you okay?"

"Yes," he called out. No, he thought.

He'd done a lot of stupid things in his life, but it had been a long time since he'd done something *this* stupid.

This was even worse than when he had to buy Carol a new pair of panty hose. And that had been in front of Lacey, too.

He didn't know what lesson God was trying to teach him. He couldn't remember praying for patience, or humility, but he was receiving big lessons in both.

He stared at Lacey in silence. She quieted, lowered her arms and stared back.

Neither of them moved until a gust of wind blowing over the water caused Randy to shiver. He gathered his composure and began to make his way back to the shore, wading through the thigh-deep water.

The closer he got to the shore, with the water becoming increasingly shallow, the more it sloshed and splashed around him.

When he reached dry ground, he stood before Lacey. Her eyes were wider than he'd ever seen. She held his cell phone at her side with one hand, and raised her other hand to cover her mouth, which was gaping open.

"That was fun," he grumbled sarcastically.

"Are you okay? You didn't hurt yourself, did you?" she asked, her voice muffled from behind her hand.

"Nothing's hurt except my pride." Not to mention any last semblance of dignity. "I hope you at least got some good pictures."

"They were just ducky," she said as she lowered her hand.

Randy stiffened and stared at her. "Ducky?" Another drip of water ran down his face. "Oh, har dee har."

Lacey snickered.

Randy watched as she thought about her own

words, and it seemed that the more she thought about it, the funnier they became, because she suddenly burst out laughing.

She lowered her voice. "The photos are just ducky, luv," she said in a very bad fake British accent. As soon as she finished her poor rendition, she started laughing again.

Randy didn't laugh. Instead, he shivered. "I might laugh about this tomorrow, but right now I'm really cold." He sniffled, then pushed back his wet hair off his face. "And I don't know what's in that water, but I don't smell too good, either."

Her laughter suddenly faded into a gasp. "I almost forgot! You have a church service to go to! We have to hurry and get you back home!"

He raised his wrist, looked at his watch, with its now-blank digital window. He tapped it, although he knew it wouldn't make any difference. He looked down at his soggy clothes and pulled his dripping keys out of his pocket, along with his drenched wallet. "Maybe you should drive," he mumbled, then shoved his wallet back into his pocket and handed her the keys.

She held out the phone, but then stopped before he touched it, and stared at his dripping clothes. "I think I'd better keep this for a while," she said as she dropped the phone into her purse. "Let's go."

While they walked back to the car, Randy listened politely without really responding as Lacey talked about the scenery, the path, the traffic, even how much she enjoyed the hot dog. She talked about everything except ducks, which Randy greatly appreciated. It was going to be a long time before he wanted to see another duck.

Besides the annoying squelching sound as he walked, the disgusting feel of soaked socks and the water that seeped between his toes at every step, he wondered if the sensation of the extra weight was similar to what Bob complained about when he talked about what it was like to wear heavy, steel-toed safety boots all day long.

By the time they got back to the car, Randy couldn't stop his teeth from chattering, and nothing he could think about could distract him from how uncomfortable he was in his wet clothes. Worse than how he felt, he didn't want to think of what he looked like. His clothes were sticking to him in some places and hanging in baggy lumps in others. After being completely submerged, he didn't want to think of what had happened to his hair.

The electronic switch to unlock the door wouldn't work after being submerged, so Lacey had to insert the key and turn it.

"Do you have a blanket or towel or anything in the car? Or better yet, a plastic bag?"

"I don't know." Randy tried to control the chattering of his teeth long enough to answer.

At his words, Lacey turned to him suddenly. Randy didn't move as she raised her hands and pressed her palms to his cheeks. "Oh! You're freezing! You should take off all that wet stuff."

He shook his head. "No. It's not that bad." A sudden chill racked his body from head to toe, completely negating his words.

Lacey shrugged out of her sweater. "Quit trying to be brave. Take off your shirt and put this on. Or at least wrap it around you. You might look a little silly, and I can't do anything about your jeans, but this is better than nothing."

While he peeled his shirt off and wrapped Lacey's purple sweater around his shoulders, Lacey rummaged through his car until she found a plastic bag he'd used for garbage and shoved under the seat and forgotten to throw out. She emptied the garbage into a receptacle, and spread the bag on the passenger seat. "Sit on that. It will save your upholstery. Hurry up. We might still be able to make it on time."

Randy complied, but he felt like a complete misfit all the way home. From the car, through the underground parking and into the lobby, he trailed little dribbles of water behind him. Lacey insisted he stand on the plastic bag in the elevator, but he still left a trail of dribbles on the carpet from the elevator to his apartment door. By the time Lacey caught up to him with the plastic bag, he was already inside his apartment. He ran straight to the bathroom and slammed the door behind him.

"The service starts in twenty-one minutes!" Lacey called out through the door.

Instead of responding with a comment, Randy jumped into the hot shower. As tempting as it was to stay in the warmth, he was out in three minutes. He tugged on the first clothes he touched, pushed his hair back, and ran back out the door with Lacey right behind him.

They ran into the church at eight minutes to the hour.

"Where were you?" Paul asked. "I called your place and there was no answer. I tried your cell, but I only got your voice mail. I almost…" Paul's voice trailed off.

"I didn't hear the phone because I wasn't wearing it and I had it set to vibrate."

Someone, probably Celeste, gasped, knowing that he never did anything without his cell phone on his belt. The only time he wasn't wearing it was when he was home, in bed, and everyone knew it.

"Your hair is wet. What were you doing?" Paul immediately looked to Lacey's hair, which was of course perfectly dry, then looked at Randy's clothes, which were not the same he'd worn that morning to the early service.

Randy gritted his teeth. "I hope you're not thinking what I think you're thinking," Randy grumbled, "because if you are, you're wrong. Everybody's honor is fully intact. Now if you'll excuse me."

He stomped off to the sound room and set the controls as best he could while his friends finished practicing the last song they would be playing for the service.

Lacey's footsteps echoed up the stairs behind him.

"Do you want to go pray with your friends before the service starts? I'll be okay to stay here."

He really didn't want to, but he knew this was a time that he really should.

"Yeah. Thanks," he mumbled as he left the sound room.

As usual, as soon as he got there everyone stood, forming a circle. They joined hands and closed their eyes to pray.

"Dear Lord," Paul began, "please bless our time together as a team, to help the people gathered here to focus on praising You tonight." Paul paused, waiting for everyone to take a turn.

"Thank You for bringing us all together once again," Adrian said softly. "And thank You for bringing Randy back safely to us."

Randy suddenly felt all choked up. Adrian knew more than any of them how much Randy hated being late for anything, and it didn't surprise Randy that Adrian would have been worried about him, especially when he didn't answer his cell phone when Paul tried to call.

Celeste's soft voice came next. "Thank You for Randy's ministry here, for bringing his, uh, friend, Lacey. I also pray that Lacey's brother-in-law's mind and heart will be open to seek You and discover Your forgiveness and blessings."

Randy nodded silently. It didn't surprise him that Celeste would be praying for Eric. Celeste was the only one besides himself who knew what that side of life could really be like, not the party-hearty escapades, but the anguish and bitter trap that lay beneath what the rest of the world saw.

Bob squeezed his hand. "I know this is changing the subject, but I really feel like praying for Randy. Dear Lord, I think Randy needs Your help and guidance right now. Please point him in the right direction, and show him plainly where You want him to go and what You want him to do."

Randy's head spun. He hadn't told anyone, but Bob didn't need to be told that Randy's life was off center. As his best friend, Bob could tell, probably even before Randy had figured it out.

"Lord God, I don't know what to say. I don't know what to do. I feel like I'm on autopilot. I came here to praise and worship You, but I feel like I've lost my focus. Even at work, I can only count how many minutes until it's time to go home. I must be getting fat, because all I can think of is how soon it's going to be until the next suppertime. My computer isn't even as much fun as it used to be, and I'm finding it hard to concentrate on stuff." He gulped.

Everyone's eyes opened, and everyone stared at him.

He turned and looked into the olive-green eyes of his best friend.

"Well," Bob said. "It's finally happened. I think Randy is in love."

Randy felt himself sway. He almost had to struggle to keep himself upright on his feet. He didn't want to entertain the possibility, but Bob's words confirmed what he feared. He'd felt it when he rose out of the water, watching Lacey screaming and waving her arms, frightened for him. As soon as she saw he hadn't drowned, his life swirled into a time warp—time had stood still, except for the pounding of his heart, as they stared at each other, Lacey on the shore, and him nearly up to his waist in the water. His life changed in that one instant. Coming up out of the water and seeing Lacey's face washed away all the reasons he'd used to enclose himself in a fishbowl of his own making.

He loved Lacey. He'd probably loved her from the first moment he met her, and he would always love her.

"It's about time," Bob said. "Go get 'er, tiger."

Paul smiled. "And the people said..."

"Amen!" everyone chorused, except Randy, and they all left the small room, leaving him all alone.

Randy stared at the whiteboard, where the Sunday school teacher who used that room had written a verse.

"There is a time for everything, and a season for every activity under heaven, Ecclesiastes 3:1."

He didn't have the whole section memorized, but the theme roared through his mind, with one section of one verse resounding like a chorus of trumpets in his brain—"a time to love."

He could take a hint, especially when God smacked him upside the head with it.

It was time to get serious with Lacey, and it was time to show her that he was the man she could love as her partner for the rest of her life, because he certainly loved her and wanted to be with her for the rest of his life.

But for now, he had a church service to attend, and it was time to get behind the scenes and serve his Lord the best way he knew how.

When he slid back into his chair in the sound room, Lacey was counting the effects buttons. "How do you keep track of all this?" she asked, her finger hovering over the last one.

If it were anyone else besides Lacey, he would have given that person a long, complicated technical explanation, knowing they didn't understand, just to impress them.

He smiled at Lacey's perplexed expression. "Experience. It's just what I like to do."

Slowly he showed her the basics, and then let her refine a few of the settings as his friends played. "You're a quick learner. You haven't given yourself enough credit. I remember that Bryce said you were afraid of computers, but that's not true. You're just inexperienced, and inexperience can be fixed."

Her cheeks darkened. "Quite honestly, I've been thinking of buying a computer lately."

His smile widened. "I happen to know just the salesman who can help you get the best one. And I bet he'll even throw in some free tech support."

Her cheeks darkened even more.

The pastor didn't use the PowerPoint displays for the evening service, so at the end of the worship time Randy escorted Lacey down the stairs, but they didn't join his friends. Instead, they sat by themselves, just the two of them. As he listened to the pastor's informal, evening-style sermon, Randy knew that this was how he wanted to spend the rest of his life—with his friends nearby and Lacey at his side.

After the service was over and the crowds mingled and socialized, he shared the last doughnut with Lacey, ignoring Adrian's raised eyebrows as he did so.

He didn't want to hang around, but because

Lacey's car was in the parking lot, she would be going straight home, alone, afterward. Therefore, Randy drew out every moment as long as he could.

He was proud of Lacey as she helped his friends pile all their equipment into the storage room.

Because it took longest to take down the drums, Bob and George were the last ones out of the building, except for Randy and Lacey, and Pastor Ron.

As Bob left, he looked at Randy and coughed a few times. George elbowed him in the ribs, then dragged him outside.

"Poor Bob," Lacey said. "Do you think he's coming down with a cold? Isn't their wedding next weekend?"

"Bob's fine. Don't worry about him. I just have to make one last check to make sure everything in the sound room is locked up, and then we can leave, too."

He walked Lacey to her car while Pastor Ron locked up the building, then drove away, leaving them all alone in the parking lot, everything around them dark.

He waited while Lacey unlocked the door, but he deliberately stood in the way so she couldn't open it to get inside.

"Lacey, before you go, we should talk. I think—"

His words were cut off as she pressed one finger to his lips.

"Shh. I know what you're going to say. It's okay.

It was just a dumb accident. Don't worry about it. But while we're talking about it, I wanted you to know something."

As she removed her finger, Randy gritted his teeth, ready to have a strip torn off him for being so reckless for going out on the slippery rocks in his leather shoes, which were now probably ruined.

"If the same thing would have happened to Eric, he would yelled and screamed and blamed Susan. I know, I've seen it happen. It wouldn't even matter if it was in front of the kids. He always makes it clear that whatever happens is Susan's fault. Even if she started crying, he'd still continue to scream at her. Then the first minute he had a chance, he would go out and start drinking, saying she drove him to it." She smiled, and her eyes shone in the reflection of the lights overhead. "You only asked about the pictures, and then we rushed off to church—we even made it without being late. Oh! The pictures!" She stopped talking and began to dig through her purse. "I almost forgot to give you back your cell phone."

Randy accepted it, pressed it to the waistband on his pants, then froze as he felt his cheeks heat up in a blush, which seemed to be happening a lot lately. "Oops. I changed so fast, I didn't grab my belt. Besides, it was pretty wet. The clip for my phone is still lying on the bathroom floor with everything else." He simply dropped the phone into his pocket.

"I'm sorry I laughed at you, but you were so funny. I'm really glad you weren't hurt. That's too bad about your watch."

He shrugged his shoulders. "I can buy a new one. It's not a big deal."

Lacey stepped closer, raising one hand to touch his shoulder. "You are a decent man, Randy Reynolds."

Before he could respond, she rose up on her tiptoes, leaned forward and brushed a gentle kiss to his lips.

Randy closed his eyes, enjoying the moment, but it was too short. When she lowered herself, Randy couldn't take the separation. He reached forward and cupped her face in his palms. "Lacey," he muttered as he lowered his head "I, uh…I…" He brought his lips to hers and finished his sentence, whispering with their lips touching. "I like you a lot." And then he kissed her with all the love in his heart and soul. She stiffened only for a brief second, then melted into him.

Randy's heart pounded and he couldn't breathe. He wondered if this was what it was like to die and go to heaven. He released her face, and wrapped his arms around her back, kissing her fully, not stopping until the sound of a truck with a bad muffler passed them on the street, reminding him where they were.

They were in a parking lot.

Again.

It seemed the only times he'd ever kissed Lacey had been in parking lots somewhere.

A decent man wouldn't have been kissing the woman he loved in a parking lot. A decent man would have done something more romantic, especially since he knew that it was going to take a lot of work to show her the man he had become, versus the pathetic creature he once had been. God had pulled him out of the pit, and he had to prove to Lacey that he was going to stay out of the pit.

She looked up into his face, still wrapped in his arms.

Her voice came out in a husky whisper. "I guess I'll see you at work tomorrow."

This time he released her and stepped back.

"Yeah. Tomorrow. Work."

He stood where he was, not walking to his own car until Lacey's car was out of sight.

Chapter Nine

Lacey stopped and turned around as she left the store. "Good night, Brittany. Remember, if you have any problems, just call me."

She hadn't taken her first step into the mall when a familiar, handsome, blue-eyed face greeted her. "Hi, Lacey. Ready for supper?"

She really wasn't hungry. Actually, she hadn't been hungry since the end of the church service the previous evening.

"Well, I…"

Her voice trailed off as Randy's charming smile dropped, and he gave her the saddest puppy-dog eyes. She almost asked if he practiced his expression on widows and orphans. "Yes, of course I'm ready. I was going to say that I haven't eaten all day."

"Great. I was thinking that we'd go someplace different this time. You know, steak and seafood."

"Are you sure? That's a bit expensive."

He waved a piece of paper in the air under her nose. "But I have a coupon. I got it off the Internet. Buy one meal, get one free."

She couldn't argue with him, because she'd once used the same argument on him. She'd just received her coupon in the mail.

"Okay, but aren't you going out with Eric tonight?"

"Yes, but we still have to eat."

They left the mall, and Randy gave her directions to an out-of-the-way restaurant she'd never been to. Judging from his unfamiliarity with the staff, it appeared he hadn't been there before, either.

A waiter appeared promptly. "Can I get you folks something to drink?" He offered the liquor menu to Randy.

Randy smiled politely. "I'll just have coffee. Lacey?"

"Me, too, please."

After they'd ordered and the waiter left them alone with two steaming cups of fragrant coffee, Lacey looked up at Randy.

"Don't you find it difficult in situations like this? We usually go to family and fast-food places, where they don't serve liquor. But this place is different. It's quite nice."

Randy folded his hands in front of him on the table. "I'm not going to lie and say it's always easy, especially when I go out with a group of people and I'm the only one not drinking anything stronger than fruit juice, but life isn't always easy. I simply tell myself that God knows best. He gives good advice, but only if we follow it."

"God cautions us against alcohol abuse, but there are many instances in the Bible of people drinking wine. Jesus even drank wine."

"That may be so, but I don't believe Jesus had a problem with it. That's one of the reasons it's so hard for most people to stick to a diet."

Lacey stared at Randy. "What are you talking about?" She couldn't see his stomach with the table between them, but she knew he didn't have an ounce of fat on him. "You've probably never been on a diet in your life." Unlike herself. She'd been on more diets than she could count, and none of them ended up with a permanent goal she was satisfied with.

Randy pressed his hands over that very flat stomach. "No. I'm lucky that I have a high metabolism. But as you know, I have had a problem with alcohol. When we have a problem with something that tempts us that's bad, God says we're not merely to resist it, we're to run from it. We're to resist the devil, but my Bible version uses the word '*flee*' when dealing with temptation."

"Does it still tempt you?"

"I'll be honest with you, and realistic. Most of the

time, no, I'm not tempted, but sometimes I am. Most people don't know my history, so often people who don't know me well try to cajole me into having 'just one.' But it's a proven fact that an alcoholic can't stop at 'just one.' Maybe they can for a short amount of time, but soon one leads to two, and two leads to three, and three leads right back to the old cycles of total destruction. That's why the only answer is exactly what God says. Flee from it. Don't toy with it. Total abstinence. That's why it's sometimes easier to quit drinking than stick to a diet. It's possible to not drink, but it's not possible to not eat."

"I've never thought of it that way."

Randy reached over the table and grasped her hands in his. "You've got to believe me when I say I'm finished with all forms of substance abuse. God pulled me out of that life and set me onto solid ground. It's important that you believe me, and that you trust me. If you want, go ahead and talk to Paul, Adrian and Bob."

"That's okay. I believe you."

And it was true. For the first time, she thought she really could believe him. In all the situations they'd been in together, he'd behaved more than admirably. She couldn't help but compare him to everything she'd ever seen Eric say or do, and in every case, Randy did the exact opposite of everything Eric would have done.

She'd been very honest when she told Randy that he was a decent man.

Except, she didn't know why she'd kissed him. It wasn't even a big surprise that he'd turned the tables on her, and kissed her back in the way he had. She had to admit that she'd enjoyed it, too.

In order to distract herself, Lacey picked up her coffee mug and took a long, slow sip. Thankfully the waiter arrived with their meals, and she could change the subject.

"Is everyone ready for Bob's wedding this weekend?"

"Yup. Rehearsal is Friday, and the wedding is Saturday."

"That's two of your friends who look like they've settled down."

"Actually, I think Paul is settling down, too. He's been going out with a woman he's known for years, and it looks pretty serious. I'm really the last one left." He reached forward and wrapped his fingers around her hand. "Or maybe I'm not."

"I don't think I want to discuss this."

Randy released her hand and smiled. He was so handsome when he smiled, and now, with the candlelight from the table sparkling in his eyes, Lacey felt as if she could have melted into a little puddle on the chair.

"That's okay. We've seen each other every day for

a long time now, and we're going to keep seeing each other every day. I think you know how I feel about you, and I'm hoping that you feel the same. We'll just see how it goes."

Lacey didn't know if that was a promise or a threat.

Randy held up his coffee mug in the form of a single toast, winked and took a sip.

Lacey nearly choked. Of course she liked Randy, but the thought of falling in love with him was too frightening to consider.

Her father hadn't been drunk all the time. Most of the time he'd been a good man, and a good father and, she thought, a good husband. But when he did drink, she knew he drank a lot. Then, all it had taken was one bad episode and their lives had been changed forever.

Echoes of her mother crying and the misery of having everything in her life stripped away due to the ravages of her father's alcohol abuse roared through her. She couldn't live like that. Nor could she bear the heartache of what she saw happening to Susan; there were too many bad days compared to too few good ones—at least until Randy had started helping Eric deal with his life, and his addiction.

But Randy wasn't her father, nor was he Eric. Randy was a unique individual. Sometimes a little too unique, but those qualities in him made her love him even more.

This time Lacey did choke.

She did love him. She didn't know when it happened, but it definitely had happened.

"Lacey? Are you okay? Here, have some water."

She took a slow sip, and coughed into her napkin. "It's okay. I'm fine. I must just have a frog in my throat."

"Are you nearly done? We have to get going to Eric and Susan's pretty soon."

She quickly finished off her last bite. "I'm done. We can go. This was delicious. Thank you."

"You're welcome." Randy signaled the waiter. "The timing is perfect. I told you we'd be fine."

"By the way, while we were talking about Bob and George's wedding, I meant to ask, what should I wear?"

Randy chuckled. "You work in a clothing store. Don't tell me you don't know what to wear to a wedding."

"I just need to know if it's casual or dressy, and how many people will be attending."

"It's probably going to be a little more dressy because George's family is going to be there, as well as some friends of their family. George's parents are divorced, and she hasn't seen her mother since she was a child. I hear that George found out where her mother is, and she'll be coming, too, as well as some of her family from that side. She's pretty excited. Bob said he'd know later in the week exactly how many people are going to be there. But her father is really rich, so I guess that means some of the people there will be really dressed up." Randy pressed his palm to his chest. "Of course, I don't have to worry. I'm going to be all decked out in my rented tuxedo. Final fittings are on Thursday. I'll bet you can hardly wait to see how handsome and debonair I'm going to look."

Lacey couldn't tell if he was being serious or facetious. Although she had no doubt that he would look great in a tux. She just never intended to tell him so.

Randy looked at himself in the mirror, and straightened his bow tie. "I sure look great in this monkey suit, don't I?" He stepped back and did his best imitation of a James Bond pose.

"What are you doing?"

Randy didn't move as he replied. "It's okay, Bob. You look good, too. But you don't have to worry. You've already impressed the woman of your dreams and she's going to marry you in less than an hour. I still haven't completely impressed the woman of my dreams."

"Still, it sounds like things have been going well since last Sunday."

"Yeah. We had a little talk on Monday, and after that something changed. It's been real subtle, but it's there. I plan to ask her to marry me tonight. I figure that a wedding is pretty romantic, so this is a real good opportunity to catch her when the mood is right."

"That seems kind of fast. Are you sure you're ready for that kind of commitment?"

Randy turned to his best friend. Visions and memories of kissing Lacey danced through his head. She wouldn't have kissed him like that if she didn't mean it. And that hopefully meant she was ready to kick their relationship up a notch, too, like he was. "I'm more than ready. Your family was always good to me, but this is the one thing I've always had missing in my life and now God has given me the chance to have it. I'm going to do everything I can to make it happen."

Bob grinned. "In other words, every little bit helps, including that rented suit."

Randy wiggled the bow tie, making it crooked once again. "I've heard that nothing impresses a woman more than formal wear and good manners."

"Or a uniform. That's how I got George, I'm sure."

Randy gave Bob a playful punch in the forearm. "That's not a uniform. Those are called coveralls, and George wears the exact same ones as you do. I don't think that sort of thing would work for me because Lacey works in a ladies' clothing store. Although, the first time I met her was when I was buying panty hose." He shuddered at the thought, even still. "Now let's get out there."

The second Randy stepped outside the small room, Bob's two brothers barged past him, trapping Bob in the room with them. Once they made sure that Bob was dressed, they called out, and Bob's three sisters joined the swarm. Randy did nothing to rescue his friend. He knew it was pointless to resist. Besides, they were just trying to keep Bob busy so he wouldn't have time to be nervous.

Randy stepped into the sanctuary.

He fought the urge to wipe his sweaty palms down the legs of his spiffy rented tux.

He was probably more nervous than Bob, which didn't make any sense, but that didn't change the fact that it was true.

He spotted Lacey almost immediately. She was sitting in the same spot they'd sat in during Sunday's evening service, wearing a pretty blue dress. As he got closer, he saw that her shoes and some kind of fluffy thing she'd stuck in her hair were all the same color as the dress.

"Wow. You look gorgeous," he said as he lowered himself into the seat beside her.

Her cheeks turned the cutest shade of pink. It made him want to kiss her, except that kissing in the middle of a crowded church was no less improper than doing so in a dark, deserted parking lot. "You look pretty good yourself. But shouldn't you be somewhere else?"

"Not yet. Bob's family needs some time alone with him. If you can call being surrounded by five siblings being alone. It's actually quite a heyday in there."

Out of the corner of his eye, Randy saw Paul and Adrian appear together.

Randy stood. "Maybe you're right, it's time to get this show on the road. I'll see you later. Remember, pick the chair closest to me for the dinner. I want to make goo-goo eyes at you all night."

Her cheeks darkened again, but she didn't comment, so Randy thought that was a good time to make his exit.

He took his place at the front with his three friends, just as they'd been shown at the rehearsal. When the music changed, the bridesmaids came up the aisle, followed by George and her father.

He leaned closer to Bob. "Wow. I don't think I've ever seen George in a dress before. She's gorgeous."

Bob smiled like an idiot, not taking his eyes off his future wife. "Yeah."

Randy looked at Bob, then back to George for a minute, then watched Lacey, who was also watching George and her father walking slowly up the aisle.

Randy could see himself going all stupid over Lacey, just like that. In fact, he wanted to go all stupid like that.

He managed to hold himself together until Bob and Georgette started saying their vows.

He'd never had someone love him unconditionally before. The love and commitment between Bob and George made them almost glow, especially when Bob ever-so-gently slipped the ring on her finger.

Just as he had feared, he felt his throat tighten and his eyes began to burn. He loved Lacey down to the bottom of his heart and soul, and he wanted Lacey to love him like that, too.

He quickly wiped his eyes when he thought no one was looking, and composed himself in the nick of time as the ceremony continued.

As he knew he would have to, when the ceremony ended he stayed by Bob's side for people to take pictures alongside the church. Then, because of the warm weather and the clear sky, the photographer convinced everyone to go to the park where he could take pictures of the wedding party amongst the natural flowers and shrubbery instead of against his studio's obviously artificial backdrops.

While Randy moved around, posing under the photographer's direction, he felt the telltale scratchiness in his eyes from his allergies kicking up. As well, he could feel his breathing beginning to tighten.

He moved away from the bushes and blossoms when he didn't have to be in the current photograph, but it didn't help. There were flowers everywhere he could go. Adrian leaned closer to him when the photographer focused a series of shots on Georgette's family.

"Randy, your eyes are getting all red and you don't look very good. Did you bring anything?"

He sniffled. "No. We weren't supposed to be outside today, so I'm not prepared for this. Of course the photographer is picking all the spots with the most flowers. How much longer is this going to last?"

Adrian checked his watch. "They haven't even started taking pictures of Bob's family yet, so it's going to be a long time before you can get out of here. You're starting to look really bad. I'll be right back."

Within a few minutes, Adrian had returned with two little pills and a bottle of eye drops.

"What is this?"

"I know someone else who has bad allergies, too. She gave me these for you."

"I don't know. It's not a great idea to take someone else's meds, especially prescription stuff." Despite his hesitations he accepted the pills from Adrian. "But at the same time, it's also not a great idea for me to be like this, either. I don't want to have to leave, and I especially don't want to leave in an ambulance with a ventilator." He popped the pills into his mouth, and swallowed them dry. "Thank your friend for me."

Adrian removed the lid from the eye drops. "Want me to put these in for you, since there isn't a mirror out here?"

With Adrian making such an offer, he could only imagine what he looked like. He didn't want to ruin Bob's wedding pictures with his bloodshot eyes. "Yeah. Let's go under that tree where less people will be watching. Thanks, Adrian."

By the time the groomsmen were called back for more pictures, Randy was already starting to feel better. He made a mental note to send a gift to Adrian's friend.

After the pictures were finished and the wedding party was once again inside the building where the only flowers were fake, Randy felt completely back to his old self. He ignored everyone and everything, and went searching for Lacey.

As soon as he found her, she took him out of the way of the crowd. "Every table here has two bottles of wine on it."

"Actually, there's a bottle of wine, and a bottle of sparkling fruit juice, so people can have a choice. George's family aren't Christians except for her mother, and her father wanted the guests to be comfortable since this isn't the kind of wedding celebration they're used to attending."

She leaned closer to him. "Are you okay with that?"

"Of course I'm okay. Just like everyone here, I

have my choice, and my choice was made over six years ago. Don't worry about me. Are you okay here?

"Yes, there's a lot of people from your church who I've talked to before, so I'm not completely alone. Now go up to the head table. Bob and George are coming."

He pointed to the table nearest where he would be sitting. "I tilted that chair for you. We won't be sitting together, but we should be able to talk without having to shout. See you later."

When he took his place at the head table, Randy noticed that Paul was also walking to the head table holding hands with a woman. Paul gave the woman a quick peck on the cheek before he guided her to a chair, then walked away.

Randy's heart ached. He truly was the last one of his four friends without someone to call special, who would call him special.

Though, with a little luck and a lot of prayer, after Bob's wedding was over he hoped that would change.

Randy pulled the paper out of his pocket with the list of the order of events, and stood. As MC, he called everyone's attention to Bob and George and began the chain of events that, at the end of it all, would send Bob and George out into the world as a happily married couple.

As expected, his speech about Bob had everyone

present nearly rolling in the aisles with laughter, including those people on George's side of the family who didn't even know Bob.

To Randy's joy and relief, everything went exactly as planned. When he came to the last item on his list, again Randy stood.

"Here it is, everyone, the moment we've all been waiting for. I made a video documenting the courtship of my friend, Roberto," he said, carefully rolling the *R*'s in his best imitation of the way Bob's mother said Bob's full real name when she was angry, "and his beautiful wife, Georgette, who looks great in a dress, I must say. Now everyone can see what Paul, Adrian and I had to put up with to get to this point."

Bob's sister's boyfriend hit the switch for the lights, sending the room into sudden, total blackness. Before anyone's eyes could adjust, the bright light of the video broke the darkness, searing like a knife through Randy's head. He stared at the screen, but he couldn't see the whole picture—a glare of light with a dull gray spot in the center marred his vision.

Randy felt himself sway. He quickly sank down into the chair, landing with a thud.

"Randy? Are you okay?" asked Paul, who was sitting beside him.

He covered his eyes with his hands. "I'm not having a very good day," he mumbled as he pressed into his temples with his fingertips. "I've been feeling a headache coming on all day, I think it started with all the flowers in the park. Now the sudden light just triggered it into a migraine. I already have a blind spot and it feels like my head is going to explode."

"Do you want me to take you home?"

"I can't leave, and you can't, either. This is Bob's wedding." Randy quickly fished his keys out of his pocket and opened up the secret compartment in his keychain fob, where he always stored one of his prescription migraine pills for emergencies. "The video is going to last twenty minutes. I'm going to take my meds and go lie down in the closet where the supplies are because that's the only room without a window. Come and get me at the part where George drives the motorcycle by herself for the first time. That's three minutes before the end. That gives this just enough time to work, and I should be okay."

He quickly swallowed the pill, dumped some ice cubes from his water glass into one of the cloth napkins, and went into the pitch-black broom closet. He did his best to relax laying on what he hoped was a clean spot on the floor, with the napkin containing the ice over his eyes.

A gentle rap sounded on the door just as he felt the dulling effect of the meds starting to work.

"Randy? Time's up. You going to be okay?"

He sat up slowly, pushed himself to his feet and opened the door. He blinked repeatedly until he could get used to the harsh light before stepping out of the closet. "The headache is starting to fade, so other than feeling incredibly thirsty, I feel worlds better. Thanks. Now let's get back to the action."

Chapter Ten

Lacey joined a group of people to talk to while Randy and the rest of the wedding party visited with different people around the room.

Just as he'd teased her, he did look great in the tuxedo, and every once in a while, she'd noticed that as she was watching him, he was also watching her.

"Your name is Lacey, isn't it?"

Lacey turned to the woman who had addressed her. "Yes. I'm so sorry, I know you're one of Bob's sisters, but I can't remember your name."

"It's Maria. Don't feel bad. You're the new face here. I only had to learn one new name, but you've had to learn dozens."

"Pleased to meet you, Maria. The wedding's been beautiful. Bob and Georgette make such a nice couple."

"Yes, everything has gone so well. Even that ridiculous video Randy made was great. We weren't sure what it was going to be like. Sometimes we don't know what to expect from Randy. Speaking of Randy, why aren't you with him?"

At the mention of his name, Lacey turned her head to watch him. Randy was talking to someone different than the last time she'd looked at him, and this time, as he was speaking, he was pouring the last of the contents of one of the bottles from a nearby table into a glass.

Lacey turned back to Maria. "I don't want to stop him from doing what he should be doing. After all, he is the best man and there are people here he hasn't seen for a long time. He can see me anytime. I told him to go visit with everyone he won't be seeing for a while."

Maria moved closer. "He keeps looking at you."

"I know." She kept looking at him, too.

Maria's voice lowered to a whisper. "He likes you, you know."

Not really knowing how to respond, all Lacey did was nod.

"Randy has such a kind heart. All of us tend to watch out for him. He lived with us for a while, you know."

Suddenly Maria had all of Lacey's attention. "He's mentioned that to me. He said your mother taught him a lot about cooking."

Maria sighed. "Yes, Mama has quite a heart for

poor Randy. Maybe I'm saying more than I should, but Randy's parents left him alone so much—more than they should have, Mama always used to remind us. They traveled a lot and when they were gone, Randy stayed with us."

"Didn't he have relatives to stay with?"

"No. The few relatives he had seemed very old. Even his parents were a lot older than Mama and Papa. Mama always insisted he stay with us so he wouldn't be so sad."

Hearing the wistful tone of Maria's voice instantly made Lacey feel sad for Randy. "He never talks about his parents." Not that she told him much about her parents, either. "What did Randy's parents do that they had to travel so much?"

"I'm not really sure. All we knew was that they were self-employed. Often they were gone for months at a time, and sometimes it sounded more like vacations than business. Once they were gone for six months. That's a long time for a kid. Mama insisted Randy stay with us so he wouldn't miss school."

Lacey's head spun. "I can't imagine having seven children in the house at once."

"Our house was busy. But everyone had a job to do, including Randy." Maria turned to look at Randy, who was filling up his glass from one of the bottles from another table. He raised his head just as Lacey looked at him, making eye contact. He winked, blew her a kiss, then grinned ear to ear.

Maria giggled. "I told you he likes you." She leaned closer. "My sisters and I, even though we're younger than Bob, we always thought Randy was so handsome! And those eyes!"

Lacey couldn't stop her blush. The unique blue of Randy's eyes was what had prompted her to buy the dress she was now wearing—it was the same color as Randy's heart-stopping eyes. Then once she had the dress, it was only natural to buy accessories in the same color.

She turned again to watch Randy, but this time he wasn't watching her. He had turned around and was starting to walk back toward the head table. On his way, he bumped into someone. Randy said something, they both laughed, Randy bowed melodramatically and then continued on his way.

"It sure is crowded in here," Lacey said, compelled to make some kind of excuse for him.

"Yes. After we invited everyone, Georgette's family decided to come at the last minute, so the room is filled to the capacity of the permit."

"Who did the decorating? It's lovely. I meant to tell you earlier."

"My sisters and a few of our friends. Randy made all the banners on his computer. Didn't he do a good job? He's so creative."

Lacey gritted her teeth. Ever since she'd met Randy, everyone continually sang his praises, and now even Bob's sister was doing it. Just once she thought someone could say something slightly negative about him, but no one ever did. But then, instead of agreeing, Lacey knew she would probably defend him, which was even worse.

Randy picked up something at the table, then turned around, making a path directly for her. He had almost made it when another guest stopped him to talk.

The longer they spoke, the louder Randy's laugh became.

He swayed on his feet, laughed a little more, then turned around and again refilled his glass.

"Well," Lacey said under her breath. "He certainly seems to be having a lot of fun tonight."

Maria's head tilted to one side. "Maybe, but something seems different about him. He's not usually so…loud. Or maybe it's my imagination. I don't know."

Lacey had just been thinking the same thing. "Maybe I'll go talk to him. Excuse me."

She hadn't taken more than three steps, when someone whom she didn't recognize stopped her. "I know I've seen you somewhere before," the woman said. "You work at the mall, don't you?"

She glanced toward Randy. This time, when they

made eye contact, he started to make kissy motions with his lips at her. He nudged the man he was standing beside, pointing to her. The man nodded, reached for one of the bottles from the nearest table and topped up Randy's glass.

Randy raised the glass to his lips.

Lacey narrowed her eyes and stared at the table nearest to him. Randy was acting stranger than usual. She was too far away to tell which bottle Randy was drinking from, but the bright colors on the label of the bottle remaining on the table didn't seem to be the wine bottle.

She glared at Randy, watching him as took a sip.

Randy's eyes widened when he noticed that she was watching. He sputtered into the glass, then swiped the back of his hand over his mouth.

Busted.

She'd seen enough of Eric sneaking booze at their house when he thought Susan wasn't watching. She knew all the signs, and she also knew that the more intoxicated Eric became, the less subtle he was when he saw that he'd been caught. Now, in the same way, she'd startled Randy.

His words from the beginning of the evening echoed through her head. He'd told her not to worry, but she had worried, and rightly so.

What she feared would happen, had happened.

Randy thunked his glass onto the nearest table,

turned around and hurried to the doorway leading to the hall. No one else was coming in as he was going out, but he didn't make it all the way through the door. Randy walked into the doorframe. He bounced back and shook his head, swaying on his feet as he pressed his fingers to his temples. He shook his head, then aimed himself carefully through the center of the doorway, staggered through and disappeared down the hall.

It was all Lacey needed to see, but something deep inside of her wanted to give him the benefit of the doubt.

She strode to the glass that he'd left on the table, picked it up and sniffed it.

The sharp odor of alcohol wafted up at her.

Her stomach clenched.

He'd asked her to trust him. Just like her mother had trusted her father, which was the catalyst that led to her father's drunk-driving accident where he'd killed himself, followed by the loss of everything else they held dear until all they had between the three of them was each other. Because her father had promised to use restraint, and her mother had trusted him.

Lacey didn't know if she wanted to throw up, or cry.

But whatever she did, she wasn't going to do it here.

She walked straight to the table where she'd been

sitting, retrieved her sweater and purse and made her way to the door.

Maria stopped her before she could escape. "Lacey? Where are you going?"

"I really can't stay. Thank you for inviting me."

"It wasn't me who invited you, it was Randy. Where is Randy? Does he know you're leaving? Don't you want to talk to him?"

Lacey gulped, barely managing to fight back the burn in the back of her eyes.

"No. I don't." Not now. Not ever again. "Goodbye, Maria. It was nice meeting you."

Lacey walked away without allowing Maria to respond.

She didn't know how she got home, or how she managed to make it home without crying, but the second she closed her apartment door behind her, the tears she'd been holding back could no longer be restrained. As she cried, she wished Susan could be there for her, just like she'd been for Susan, so many times. Susan was the only one she knew who could understand. Lacey had comforted her sister so many times as Susan cried over Eric. While Lacey had always sympathized, until now she had never adequately imagined the soul-wrenching pain of the betrayal.

He'd promised. She'd wanted to trust him.

And now, just like her sister, she'd been reduced

to a pile of mush, sobbing her eyes out because she'd believed that Randy would keep his word. Yet at the same time, it was exactly what Susan had done with Eric, and continued to do, time and time again, only to be disappointed, time and time again.

Lacey couldn't live like that. By allowing Randy into her life she'd let him break down her defenses—she'd let her heart override her head, and now she was no better off than Susan, except for the fact that she wasn't married to Randy.

And she would never be married to Randy.

A fresh flood of tears burst out. For a while she'd actually imagined what it would be like to be married to Randy. He made her laugh, but now all she could do was cry, and she hated herself for it.

Randy blinked to help focus his vision. "What do you mean, she left?"

Maria pointed to the door. "She just picked up her stuff and left. She said she didn't want to talk to you. What did you do?"

Randy's head swam. "I didn't do anything."

Just to make sure that Lacey hadn't seen what he was planning to do and ran off, Randy reached into the inside pocket of his tuxedo jacket. He remembered leaving the brochure at the head table, and he remembered that he wanted to go get it before Lacey saw it, but now he couldn't remember if he actually had recovered it. He reached up to pat the inside breast pocket of his jacket, but his hand missed its mark and he smacked himself on the side of his chin.

Maria tilted her head. "What's the matter with you?"

Slowly and carefully he reached into the pocket. The brochure of engagement rings he'd picked up from the jeweler's was still in there after all, along with the Valentine card he'd managed to find out of season, that he was going to give to Lacey as a declaration of his love. "Nothing. My coordination's just a little off." And his head was swimming, but the headache and nausea were at a level he could handle and still talk to people coherently, even if he was having trouble concentrating.

Adrian appeared at his side. "I just saw Lacey in the parking lot. She got into her car and drove away."

Randy sighed. "I know."

Adrian pulled him to the side. "Excuse us, Maria. I need to talk to Randy alone. You know. Guy stuff."

Maria smiled, satisfied, and walked away.

"What's the matter with you? I saw you walk into the door frame a few minutes ago, and then you ran into the washroom faster than you've ever moved on the basketball court. Are you feeling sick?"

"I had a migraine coming on, so instead of going home, I took one of those new meds my doctor gave me. My coordination's off a little more than usual." He rubbed his chin where he'd just smacked himself. "But at least I got to take my meds before I got sick this time."

"Then why were you running?"

Randy grinned, proud of himself for his ingenuity. "I'm usually very careful to always pour my own drinks, but I let someone else top up my glass, and he poured wine into it. I spit it out, but I didn't want the taste in my mouth, so I went to go brush my teeth."

"Brush your teeth? Here? You've got a toothbrush in your pocket?"

He smiled brightly, knowing his teeth were white and shiny, and sparkling clean as any toothpaste commercial. "Yeah. I bought one of those small fold-up, travel kinds. It even comes with a small tube of toothpaste. I was planning on, uh, well, never mind." He sighed, and all the joy seeped out of him. He was planning on getting up close and personal with Lacey tonight, to propose to her on bended knee, and he wanted everything to be perfect, including clean and minty fresh breath. Not only were things not going perfect, they weren't even going well.

He stared at the doorway. "She's gone. I don't know what happened. I barely even talked to her all night. Do you think she's mad because she thinks I'm ignoring her?"

Adrian shook his head. "You're crazy. You're carrying a toothbrush, but you didn't bring anything for your allergies…" Adrian's voice trailed off, and his brows knotted. "Wait a minute. Did you just say you took something for a migraine?"

Randy pressed his fingers into his temples. "Yeah. But I feel better. Except I feel more spaced-out than usual after I take my meds." He didn't tell Adrian that the side effects of the strong medication that made him feel loopy at the best of times were getting worse and worse as time went on. "It must be the new prescription. I'm going to have to go back to the old kind, even though they're more expensive."

"Did you forget about the stuff I gave you at the park for your allergies?"

"Of course not, but no one has ever seen me when I'm down with a migraine and I want to keep it that way." He especially didn't want Lacey to ever see him like that. Over the years he'd spent too many hours lying on the bathroom floor with the dry heaves, feeling like his head was going to explode. That was why he spent the extra money on a very luxurious plush mat for the bathroom.

"Randy?"

"Oops. Sorry. I was thinking about something else."

"You're acting really strange."

"I'm feeling kind of strange, too. But I'm still handsome in this monkey suit."

"You're getting worse. Maybe you should go lie down. Or better yet, everything's almost over. You should go home."

"But I have to help clean up."

"In your condition, I think you'd be more a hazard than a help. Go home."

"I don't want to go home."

"Randy…"

As Randy looked at his friend, his vision blurred briefly. He concentrated to refocus. "I don't want to go home without Lacey. I have to find her before midnight, before I turn into a pumpkin."

Adrian grabbed his arm. "That does it." Adrian turned to the side. "Paul, can you come here for a minute?"

"What?"

"We've got to find someone to take Randy home."

"Okay. Fine," Randy grumbled. He reached into his breast pocket for his keys, but they weren't there. He reached into one pants' pocket, then the other before he finally found them. He saluted, and valiantly handed his keys to Adrian. "See. I'm smart enough to know I shouldn't be driving. It says so right on the bottle. I always read the labels, even though I'm not allergic to peanuts."

Adrian returned the keys. "That's fine to not drive, but how do you think you're going to get into your apartment without your keys?"

"Oops. I never thought of that."

Adrian sighed. "You're not thinking much about anything right now." Adrian turned to Paul. "I changed my mind. I don't think it's a good idea to let him go home alone. I think I'll take him to my place, and he can camp out on my couch for the night."

"Good idea," Paul said.

"But I have to see Lacey! I can't let the sun go down on her anger."

"You shouldn't let the sun go down on *your* anger."

"But I'm not angry. Lacey's angry."

"We don't know for sure that she's angry. But we do know that you should go lie down. Why don't you go sit over there? Everyone's starting to leave. Then we'll clean up and you come home with me."

"No. I have to go to talk to Lacey." Randy shook his head; except when he stopped shaking his head, the movement didn't stop. His vision blurred even worse than the first time. He started to lose his balance, and there was nothing he could do to stop it. He felt himself going down, out of control, just like at the duck pond. The landing had been soft then, because he'd landed in the water. Randy didn't want to drown today, either, so he held his breath.

Adrian and Paul held him, each hanging on to one arm to steady him until he could stand on his own.

"Thanks. You guys saved my life. Did you feel that earthquake?"

"Next he's going to say the sky is falling," Paul grumbled.

Randy looked up. "Then I have to find Lacey really fast, before she gets hurt."

"You're not going anywhere," Adrian said. "By the way, have you got fifty dollars I can borrow?"

Randy patted all his pockets. "Nope. I don't have any money. I didn't bring my wallet."

"You brought a toothbrush, but you didn't bring your wallet?"

"Toothbrush?" Paul asked. "That's different. Even for you."

"All I needed was my driver's license. The toothbrush pack and my wallet made a big lump in my pocket, and I needed the toothbrush more than I needed the money. I'm sorry. I can't even write you a check."

Paul turned to Adrian and reached for his own wallet. "I don't think I have that much on me. What do you need it for?"

"I don't need it. I just wanted to make sure Randy didn't have any money on him, so he couldn't sneak off and take a cab home." Adrian guided Randy to a chair. "Stay here until I come and get you. Better yet, put your head down and have a nap."

Randy did as he was told, but the second Adrian and Paul weren't looking, Randy took off and ran out the door, this time being very careful and putting both hands on the door frame as he passed through the center.

He ran through the parking lot, straight for his car.

Randy knew he was in no shape to drive, but he had something in his car that he didn't have in his pocket.

He couldn't take a cab with no money, but he had an ashtray full of coins that would be more than enough to take the bus.

Even though he hadn't taken a bus for years, today he had to take the chance that he'd be okay, and that he'd make it all the way to Lacey's apartment. Before the sun went down on her anger, he had to tell her how much he loved her.

Chapter Eleven

Lacey stood on the balcony, looking in the direction of Randy's church, where Bob's wedding had been.

It was a wonderful group of people, but she would never go back there again.

She didn't know why she'd done it, but after she'd cried herself out, she couldn't stop herself from going into the living room and studying the picture grouping containing twelve frames in sequence selected from the video of Randy falling into the water at the duck pond.

He'd given it to her as a gag gift, along with a beautiful framed and matted picture of the male and female ducks, whom Randy claimed were happily mated, until death do them part.

They'd laughed so much about him falling into the water; at least they had the next day. Randy claimed that it was a sign from God that he was to buy the printer he had his eye on, because every frame he printed came out with the quality of a real photograph.

Not that she didn't believe in signs, but she knew it was just an excuse to buy the printer, and told him so. All he'd done was laugh and buy the printer anyway.

Even though the play-by-play starting with Randy trying to feed the ducks, ending with him landing in the water, complete with one photo of just the splash, was only meant as a joke, she'd hung it right alongside the professionally framed picture of the pair of ducks.

Randy was a man who could fall down, get up, come out smiling and move forward.

The world needed more people like Randy.

Except, this time, he'd fallen and she couldn't bring herself to go help pick him up. The same thing had devastated her mother for as long as she could remember, and she'd been through it too many times with Eric and Susan. She wouldn't open herself up to being hurt like that. She refused to be a victim like her mother, and like Susan.

Lacey watched from above as a bus slowed and came to a halt at the bus stop in front of her apartment building's main entrance.

Her heart nearly stopped when a man dressed in a tuxedo stepped out, and the bus continued on its way.

She stared from above, but he didn't look up. Just like in a scene from a B-grade movie, he staggered to the lamppost and hung on to it with both arms, hugging it as he leaned, the whole time keeping his head hanging low.

Even from the height of six stories, she saw his body lurch as one hand left the pole and he pressed it to his mouth. Suddenly he pushed himself away, ran to the bushes on the property line, bent at the waist and began to throw up.

Just watching him made Lacey feel sick.

She stepped back inside, but the mental picture haunted her.

She didn't want to get involved. She couldn't go through that.

But she couldn't leave him out there. Self-inflicted by the evils of alcohol or not, Randy was sick and he needed someone, and the only someone who was going to help him was her.

She made her way down the elevator partly wishing it would stop, and partly wishing it would go faster.

When she joined Randy, he was hunched over with his palms pressed onto his knees, gasping for breath.

"Randy? It's me. Lacey. Are you going to be okay?"

"Go away. I didn't want you to see me like this."

A strange reaction. Eric always demanded that Susan help him, and most especially, clean up after him.

"I'm not leaving you out here. Come inside. I mean it."

He stood, and his pained expression told her how awful he was feeling. They walked slowly to the elevator, but when Lacey raised her hand to push the button, Randy's hand enveloped hers.

"Wait. I don't know if I can take the motion of the elevator yet. Not after the bus. I'm so sorry." He closed his eyes and leaned his back against the wall, his breathing labored.

She waited until he stood on his own, then pressed the button. At the first lurching movement of the elevator, Randy's face paled, and he staggered slightly. He clenched his teeth and fell back against the wall, then grappled with the bar that went around the three solid walls of the interior as if he were hanging on for dear life.

"I don't feel very good...."

Lacey feared for the worst, but at that moment the movement stopped and the door swooshed open. Randy drew in a deep breath and stepped out, almost swooning.

As drunk as she'd seen Eric, he'd never been as bad as Randy was now.

The second she opened her apartment door, Randy stepped inside, kicked off his shoes and ran for the washroom. The door slammed closed, and she didn't want to, but some demented part of her made her approach it. The question if he was going to be okay almost came out, but instead of the sound of wretching, which was what she'd expected, came the sounds of what seemed to be Randy brushing his teeth.

She cringed, thinking about him using her toothbrush. She should have been angry, but she couldn't be. Despite his condition, he'd seemed embarrassed outside. She couldn't begrudge him her toothbrush.

The door opened. Randy held up a toothbrush she didn't recognize. "Don't worry. I brought my own. See? I got it at the sidewalk sale."

"What are you doing carrying around a toothbrush?"

"It's a long story." He folded it up, slipped it inside a small plastic case, tucked the case in the pocket of his tuxedo jacket and stepped toward her. "But now I can be closer to you and not have to worry about being disgusting. I think God really does have a sense of humor."

Lacey backed up a step, but didn't comment.

"Lacey, we need to talk. I need to know why you ran away from me."

"You're drunk," she croaked out.

"No. I'm…" Randy shook his head a couple of times while he spoke, but his words trailed off. He stopped moving his head, swayed and his eyes widened and became glazed.

He bumped into the wall, continuing to lean on it for support. "No. I'm not."

"You could have fooled me."

"It's not what it looks like. I didn't want to get sick."

"You're sick all right, but I don't feel sorry for you when it's self-inflicted."

"No." He reached forward, toward her hands. "Not like that. I've always gotten sick on the bus. I meant—"

"Don't you dare touch me," Lacey ground out from between clenched teeth. "Don't forget, I've heard it all and seen it all from Eric, and from my father. I may have only been a kid, but I saw a lot more than they thought I did. I wouldn't want any child to have to live with those kinds of memories. Especially not a child of mine."

"But—"

"It's not open for discussion."

"I—" Again, Randy reached for her hands and stepped forward, but Lacey sidestepped him. When his hand moved forward into the empty spot, his whole body leaned forward with his hand and kept moving.

Randy fell flat on his face.

"I've fallen and I can't get up," he said not moving from his prone position with his face pressed against the carpet. "Can I stay here? I promise I'll be good. I'm housebroken. I really am. I'm cute, too."

Since he wasn't moving, Lacey didn't know if he meant stay on the floor, or stay at her apartment. She wanted to send him home, but she didn't think he'd be safe going alone in his present condition. But if he couldn't take the movement of the elevator, she certainly wasn't going to risk taking him home in her car. To his credit, at least he had been responsible enough to take the bus and not drive his car in his present condition.

She stood above him and looked down. He turned his head to the side so his nose wasn't pressed into the carpet, but he didn't get up. Instead he closed his eyes and the corner of his mouth turned up into what seemed like a lazy half smile. "Your carpet is nice and soft. Like lying on a cloud. Just like that commercial. Except there's no angels. Did you know that all the angels in the Bible were really men, none were women? Although they did kinda wear dresses. I don't wear dresses, but I'm wearing a nice tuxedo. Do you like it?"

He'd looked very handsome in the tuxedo…when he was upright. But she wasn't going to tell him that. "Are you going to get up?"

She continued to watch him, but he didn't move. Except the longer she waited, the more his body relaxed.

After a few minutes, Lacey gave up waiting for him to respond. "I guess you can stay, but…"

A soft snore interrupted her words.

"I don't believe this," she muttered.

From across the room, Lacey's cell phone rang inside her purse. She jogged across the room and answered it.

"Hi, Lacey. This is Adrian. We lost Randy. Is he there?"

She looked at Randy, who hadn't moved, which wasn't necessarily a bad thing. "Yes. He's here."

Adrian breathed a sigh of relief. "I'm glad, because that means he made it safely. I guess you can see that he's not in very good shape."

"You can say that again."

"Don't tell him I called, but I'll be right there to come and get him. I just need your address."

Because she didn't want to take Randy home in her own car in case he was sick again, she didn't think that was a good idea to take the same risk with Adrian's car.

Randy snored again.

"I think he's settled down, so it's probably best to leave him where he is."

"As long as you're sure."

She wasn't sure, but she didn't know what else to do.

"We'll be fine."

"Thanks, Lacey. I owe you. Bye."

Lacey sighed and returned to Randy's prone body. She lowered herself to kneel beside him and lightly shook one shoulder. "Wake up. You can stay here tonight, but I think you'll be better off on the couch. Randy?"

His eyes fluttered open, so Lacey held on to one

arm and tugged, in order to help him up. With her help, he pushed himself to his knees, but again he swayed, tipped and fell into her. On impact he wrapped his arms around her.

Leaving them facing each other kneeling, almost nose to nose, wrapped in each other's arms.

Randy grinned. "Just one kiss. Make me see fireworks."

"That does it. You're on your own." She pushed him away, and this time he fell onto his side.

Lacey stood. "You can stay, but I'm leaving. Just remember, by the time I get back to get ready for church you'd better be gone, both from my home and from my life."

She left quickly, not bothering to grab her sweater.

Just in case he somehow managed to get to his feet and try to follow her, Lacey ran for the stairwell. She walked down a flight of stairs, then got into the elevator from the fifth floor to go into the underground parking.

The only place she could think of to go was Susan's house, although she didn't know what she could say.

She knocked softly on Susan's door, almost wishing that Susan would send her home.

"Lacey? What are you doing here? Wasn't tonight Randy's friend's wedding?"

"Yes, but it's all over now." In more ways than one.

"Have you been crying? Come in!"

Before she realized what she was dong, Lacey spilled the whole sordid tale to her sister, including the part about falling in love with a man whom she knew would hurt her time and time again.

"I can't believe what you're telling me. Something just doesn't seem right. You should hear the things Eric has been saying about Randy. His dedication, his strong faith. His strength and determination. I can't believe he fell away. Are you sure about this?"

"I didn't want to believe it. But I saw him put the glass down, and I picked it up right away. It was wine. And he's so out of it. You know how he jumps quickly from topic to topic when he gets started on something. He's ten times worse that usual."

"Usually that's a sign of high intelligence."

"Or insanity."

"You know what I mean. I'll let you stay here under one condition."

"Name it."

"That you don't go back to our old church in the morning, that you go one more time to Randy's church and talk to his friends. Something's really bugging me about this, but I can't put my finger on it. But right or wrong, you should really take a hard look at what you're throwing away. Sometimes God wants us to take the bad with the good, because ultimately, God can use it for a purpose. We just can't see it right away. Sometimes we never will, until after we're dead and in His presence."

Lacey had been taught that concept in Sunday school, but she'd never had to actually apply it to anything in her life. It was a very difficult lesson.

"I'm waiting for your answer, Lacey."

"Since when did you become so assertive? You always used to back down in any confrontation, even if you weren't the one who was wrong."

"It's something Randy taught me, and he's right. I'll go get you a blanket and a pillow. It's time to get to bed, and I'll be seeing you in church in the morning."

Bob Delanio had just tucked the crash cymbal into its tote when a woman's voice sounded behind him.

"Bob? What are you doing here? Isn't this supposed to be your honeymoon?"

He stood and turned around. "Hi, Lacey. We're not leaving until tonight. George's mother is in town just for the weekend, so when we booked our flight, we took that into consideration."

"Oh, that's good. Listen, I hate to do this to you, but did you hear about what happened last night?"

"A little bit. Why?"

"I know you've been good friends with Randy since you were little kids. I wanted to ask you a few questions, if that's okay."

"I won't betray something told to me in confidence, but I'll do my best to answer anything else."

"Do you know why he has a drinking problem? Did he have a bad childhood, or was he affected by some tragedy?"

He looked up to the sound room, where he could see Randy turning everything off. He'd noticed that Lacey hadn't been up there with him during the service. "I think this is something you should be speaking about to Randy, not me."

"I tried, but he won't talk about it."

"Well…" Bob turned to the side as he continued to pack up his drum set, so he couldn't actually see Randy as he was talking about him. He didn't want to tell Lacey anything Randy didn't want her to know, but he could tell Lacey what he saw from his own perspective, and then she could be her own judge and draw her own conclusions.

"I don't remember anything tragic, as you say, and I wouldn't say he had a bad childhood, but if there were ever two people who shouldn't have had kids, it was Randy's parents. Maybe he was an afterthought, I don't know. But he was always left alone so much and it ate at him. I guess you've learned that Randy is quite a social animal."

"Yes. He seems to know people everywhere. And if he doesn't, he gets to know them quickly."

"Yet, he was quiet as a kid. He would brood for

days when his parents forgot his birthday, which, unfortunately, was often. Nothing any of us could do made any difference. Mama used to throw huge birthday parties for him when he was with us on his birthday. Bigger than ours." He smiled. "But none of us minded. We knew that a big party didn't make up for him being away from his family."

"Maybe it was hard for them to call from wherever in the world they were. Communications were a lot different twenty years ago than they are today."

Bob grinned. "Yeah. I think Randy has every electronic communications device known to man. Maybe that's why. Have you seen his cell phone?"

Lacey smiled back. "Of course."

Bob's smile faded. "I tried to tell him that the first time, that they must have not had access to international long distance, or that it was too expensive, and he kind of went along with it, but the next year they forgot his birthday, too, and they were home that year. They actually forgot a lot. I don't know how. They also kept promising that one day they'd get him a dog, and they never did. I don't think Randy ever got over that. Why are you asking about Randy's drinking?"

"Because of yesterday."

"He wasn't drunk. I heard that he had a bad reaction to some medication."

"That may be true, but I know he was drinking. I smelled it."

Bob's movements froze for a few seconds. "Really? I find that almost impossible to believe. It doesn't seem right."

"I'm not lying."

"I'm sorry, I didn't mean it that way, but it just doesn't make sense. You should have seen him when we were practicing. He was devastated that you wouldn't talk to him. I remember what he was like when he was hungover, even though it's been a number of years. He wasn't like that this morning. He's a little slow on the draw today, but otherwise he seemed fine." Just so sad, which normally wasn't like Randy at all. For the first time, he hadn't seen Randy singing while the worship team was practicing before the service. Randy didn't know that Bob knew what he did up there, but the drums were on a platform, so he was a bit higher up than the rest of the worship team, and he could see better across the sanctuary and into the sound booth window.

It was very telling that Lacey didn't look any happier than Randy did.

"He was sick and everything last night."

Bob shrugged his shoulders. "I would have expected that. He gets the worst motion sickness I've ever seen. As kids, and even in our teens, I can't count the times we all had to get off the bus and wait while Randy was sick. Some of the bus drivers knew us and let us on for free, but often we had to pay a second fare midtrip. I know we shouldn't have, but when that happened we always made Randy pay us back out of his allowance."

"That's awful."

"We were kids and we didn't have much money. But he got us back. He was the first one to get his driver's license and a car, and he always made us pay for gas. Kids usually grow out of the motion sickness, but Randy never did."

Bob smiled at the memories, but his smile quickly faded. "I also remember that he was the first of us to experiment with drinking, except his parents never caught him. Either that, or they couldn't be bothered enough to do anything about it. Looking back, I wonder if that's why he overdid it so much. He was just waiting for someone besides us guys to care enough to tell him to stop, and no one ever did."

"That's so sad."

"I don't know. He seems to have gotten his act together. It just took a while."

Bob purposely didn't mention the death of Randy's friend on what was the last day that Randy ever had a drink. He didn't want Lacey to feel sorry for Randy. He just wanted Lacey to love Randy. Bob knew that Randy definitely loved Lacey.

Bob hadn't seen his friend so torn up since the one-year anniversary of Karl's death. Randy hadn't turned back to drinking then, and Bob didn't think Randy would now.

"All I can say is that you should talk to him and listen to what he says. Randy is a really nice guy, and all of us think you're perfect for each other."

"You do? You've been talking about us?"

He couldn't hold back his grin. "That's what friends are for. Now if you'll excuse me, I have to finish up. And speaking of Randy, here he comes."

Lacey stiffened. "I, uh, think I should be going."

She turned, dashed off the stage and disappeared through the main door.

Bob sighed. Maybe not today, but tomorrow was another day, especially when the two of them worked next door to each other.

He paused for a minute, and prayed for God's will to happen.

Chapter Twelve

"What's the matter, loverboy? Why so glum?"

Randy wanted to tell Carol mind her own business, but being miserable was no excuse to be rude.

"I just didn't have a very good weekend. So drop it, okay." He started piling a new shipment of phones onto the shelves, probably pushing them harder than he needed to.

"Whoa! Take it easy! Want to talk about it?"

Not with Carol he didn't. "No. Why don't you just leave me alone?"

As usual, Carol didn't take the hint. She stepped in front of the shelf he was trying to stock. "What did you do?"

"I didn't do anything."

"Are you sure? She must at least think you did something."

"She thinks I was drinking again."

"Oh."

For one of those rare moments in her life, Carol was silent.

But not for long. "Well? Were you?"

"Of course not."

"Then why would she think you were?"

"I don't know." Although he knew he'd been acting strange from the combination of the allergy and the migraine medications, something in hindsight he knew he never should have mixed, but he'd needed both at the time. He'd taken a risk, and it had backfired on him. He remembered waking up on the carpet in Lacey's hallway, and he couldn't remember how he had gotten there. But he did remember getting sick on the bus, and Lacey dragging him inside.

He bowed his head and pinched the bridge of his nose. "Okay, I do know why she would have thought that. But it wasn't what it looked like."

"What did it look like?"

He lowered his voice to barely above a whisper, forcing the words out, because saying them out loud forced him to admit it was true. "It looked like I was drunk. But I wasn't."

He couldn't blame Lacey for thinking the way she did, especially after all she'd seen in her family.

"Did you tell her that?"

"Not at the time. I was pretty incoherent, and then

I was sick. And now she won't answer my phone calls. She left me a text message that she never wants to see me again."

"But that's based on a misunderstanding, isn't it? Or were you really drinking? Even just a little?"

"Of course not," he barked. "I told you that already. Why does everyone always think the worst of me?"

"Actually, no one really does. I think you just think they think that. Yikes, now I'm even beginning to sound like you! If the same thing happened to me, what would you tell me to do?"

"I'd tell you that life is too short and too fragile to give up because of misunderstandings. I'd tell you to stand up for yourself and go make it right."

"Okay. Then do it. Go. I'll cover for you."

"Pardon me?"

"You said she won't answer your phone calls, so that means you have to talk to her in person. I happen to know she's the only one in the store right now, so you have, as they say, a captive audience. Now go get 'er, tiger."

"Someone else said that to me recently. I can't remember who."

"Then that means we're right. Now go."

"And do what?"

Carol laughed. "I know you. You'll think of something."

Randy stepped outside the store, but instead of

going next door into Lacey's store, he stopped to think. What did he really want? He wanted more than just to absolve himself. He also wanted more than to tell Lacey that he loved her. He wanted the same thing he'd wanted when he was getting ready for Bob's wedding, and that was a wedding of his own.

His hand drifted to his back pocket, to his wallet, where he'd stashed the Valentine card he'd meant to give Lacey, then never did.

Despite the poem he'd written declaring his love, an out-of-season greeting card wasn't enough.

Instead of turning to go to Lacey's store, Randy turned the other way.

He meant to go to the jeweler's to get a new engagement ring brochure that wasn't creased, but his feet skidded to a halt in front of the men's specialty store. He'd wanted to impress Lacey in the rented tuxedo, but Bob's wedding was over and he'd taken it back. However, nothing was stopping him from getting another one. Maybe even something a little more fancy and special, to show her how special she was. She certainly deserved to be treated special, especially after he'd acted like such an idiot in front of her.

It was hard to find something he liked in his size that didn't need alterations, but before too long,

Randy was dressed in a full tuxedo, complete with tails and even a top hat for a final touch.

He walked into the jeweler's, picked up another brochure for a selection of engagement rings, waved at the manager and strode out.

Rather than take a chance with his allergies, instead of going to the florist, Randy's next stop was the craft store.

He didn't have a lot of time to search for what he wanted, so he walked straight to the counter. "I'd like a silk red rose, please. One of those good ones that looks real. I don't need a bag."

The woman looked him up and down, taking in every inch of his rented finery. "Would you like me to snip the price tag off and tie a lace ribbon around it for you? That would look really nice."

"That sounds like a great idea. Thanks." He smiled, then hesitated. "Or do you think that might be overdoing it a little?"

Again, she looked at the tuxedo, then up at his top hat. "No, I don't think so. It would be perfect."

In only a few minutes, Randy continued on. He made a short stop to rummage through his backpack in his own store, ignoring Carol as she stared at him. He paused for a second to calm his nerves then and walked to the entrance of Lacey's store.

Randy quickly scanned the interior. Relief flooded through him that currently there were no customers in the store. Lacey's back was to the entrance as she took advantage of the lull to unpack a selection of panty hose from a box and sort them into the slots.

Somehow, the location for what he was about to do seemed fitting.

"I'll be right with you," she said, turning her head as she spoke. "I just have to—"

At the sight of him, the box dropped to the floor. Packages of panty hose scattered around her feet.

Randy held the rose in front of him and tipped the top hat with his other hand as he approached her. "Hi, Lacey."

Her voice came out in a hoarse croak. "What are you doing here like that?"

Randy smoothed down the lapel of the jacket. "I think that should be obvious. I came here to court you."

Her eyes widened, and she scanned him from head to toe, from the top of his rented top hat, to the toes of his new leather shoes.

He reached into the inside breast pocket of the jacket, pulled out his portable CD player, set it on top of one of the racks and hit play.

Sounds of romantic music began to play softly.

Still holding the rose, he handed her the Valentine card.

"It's not Valentine's Day. It's not even close."

"I know. But that doesn't change the fact that

those words come from my heart. I wrote that poem myself. For you."

Lacey began to cough, then cleared her throat. Randy waited while she read the card. He could tell when she got to the part where he'd written "I'll love you forever" because she made a little gasp.

"We have to talk. I know what it looked like at the wedding, but I wasn't drunk at Bob's wedding. It was a bad mix of medications that I shouldn't have taken at the same time."

Her eyes narrowed. "When you ran off, I checked the drink you left on the table. It was wine. I smelled it."

Randy froze. "You did what?"

Her cheeks darkened, and she wouldn't look at him as she spoke. "You were acting so strange, and I saw you drinking an awful lot, so I checked out what was in your glass. It was wine. The real kind."

"I was drinking the sparkling fruit juice all night. I usually don't let anyone put anything in my glass, but I do admit that I wasn't myself, and I let someone else top it up without paying attention. I took one mouthful, but I spit it out, then ran to the bathroom to brush my teeth."

"You went to brush your teeth? In the middle of a wedding? Do you always carry a toothbrush?"

Randy squeezed his eyes shut for a couple of seconds. He had a feeling he was never going to hear the end of the one day he had a toothbrush in his pocket. If he ever did the same thing again, he vowed to himself that he would never tell anyone, for any reason.

"It seemed like a good idea at the time," he said quietly, then cleared his throat. "It's a long story. But the point is that I didn't drink anything."

"But you passed out on my floor. And you were sick. Although Bob told me that you still get motion sickness."

Randy's cheeks burned. "I don't like people to know that. It's kind of embarrassing."

"The point is that you passed out cold, lying on the floor. And then when I woke you up, you wrapped yourself around me and tried to kiss me."

The burn in his cheeks extended to his ears. In the back of his mind, now that she mentioned it, he kind of remembered something. If not the actual experience, he remembered the overwhelming need to kiss her, and then it didn't happen.

"Then we must have been very close. You should have been able to smell alcohol on my breath. But you didn't."

"No. All I could smell at the time was toothpaste. It was only a couple of seconds. All I know is that you were acting very drunk, and the glass you were drinking from contained alcohol. What am I supposed to think?"

Randy's hands fell to his sides. "There's a good reason for that. I have really severe allergies. That's why Bob and George didn't have any real flowers for the wedding. Everything was fake, including her bouquet. They did that for me. We'd made arrangements to go to a studio for the pictures, but the weather was so nice the photographer convinced everyone to go to the park. I didn't have anything on me, so I took someone else's allergy prescription. It got me over the hump, and I thought everything was going to be fine."

"You forgot your medication, but you brought a toothbrush?"

Randy ignored that little aside. "Then at the wedding, the abrupt change of lighting when the video started, when I was already on the verge of a whopping headache, triggered a migraine."

"One of my staff gets migraines. She's called in sick because of them. I've never had a headache so bad I've had to miss work."

"A few people know about my allergies, but only Bob, Paul, Adrian and Bob's family knows about the migraines. I don't want anyone to know. I get what's called a 'classic' migraine. First there's a flash of light, then I get a blind spot in my vision, which is surrounded by this glowing glare. I can't think of any better way to describe it. That quickly becomes a headache, and it escalates until it gets so bad I get sick. Sometimes I can't even move. There is no cure, and no one really knows what causes them. I have these very expensive migraine meds that I take only in case of an emergency, or if it's so bad I want to die. I took one so I wouldn't ruin Bob's wedding. After all, I was the best man and MC. I was okay for a while, but it caught up with me, and you saw the end results."

Lacey raised her hands to her cheeks. "Oh, Randy! That's awful! I feel so sorry for you."

Randy's face burned. "Don't. I don't want you to feel sorry for me. I didn't want you to know at all."

"Why not? Lots of people get migraines."

"Because it's just one more weakness, and I have enough weaknesses." He still held the rose in one hand, but he rammed his free hand into his pants pocket. "The drinking is bad enough, and I thought I'd been able to put it behind me. I do what I can to help others battle with it, but every once in a while, something comes back to haunt me. I know what it looked like, and I can see why you feel the way you do, so all I can do is to say that I'm telling the truth, and I'm asking you to believe me." Randy sank down onto one knee, removed the top hat, pressed it over his heart and held the rose out toward Lacey. "And I want you to love me back, warts and all, the same way I love you. And that would be the forever kind of way. But first you have to trust me."

"Trust you…" Her voice trailed off.

"Yes, Lacey, this is what it's all about. Even if you love me the same way I love you, which I hope you do, what it all comes down to is trust. If you can't trust me then we have nothing, and I'll never bother you again. This has to be an all-or-nothing thing. What do you say?"

Randy's heart pounded so hard he felt lightheaded as he waited for her reply. It was a question he didn't want to ask, but that didn't change the fact that it was the only way. He couldn't be happy in a relationship knowing she didn't trust him, that she would always have doubts when something went wrong, because in life, sometimes things did go wrong. He needed her confidence, and needed to know that he would have her full support when he struggled with the problems life threw at him. He also knew Lacey couldn't be happy or comfortable over the long term if she was always worried that he was going to fall off the wagon.

"This is so hard. You have to understand what I've been through. The things I've seen. I can't live like that."

"You won't have to live like that because I'm not like that. But what I say doesn't matter. You have to trust me, and trust that God is here, with us, and that He's always there to help. All we have to do is ask. I do that all the time." In fact, he was doing that right now.

"Don't talk. Let me think."

He expected her to say that she was going to need a few days, and he would have given her those few days. But instead of backing up, she stepped forward, accepted the rose and ran the fingers of her other hand over his cheek.

Randy closed his eyes and tipped his head, as if he could intensify the contact by leaning his face into her palm.

"This is a proposal, isn't it?"

His eyes sprang open, and he looked up at Lacey as she stood, looking down at him. Randy remained with one knee on the floor. He pulled the brochure for the engagement rings out of his pocket. "Yes, it is."

"I suppose you consider this traditional, don't you?"

She motioned her hand, encompassing the silk flower, complete with the shiny red ribbon, the top hat, his CD player, still crooning a modern rock ballad from its perch on top of one of the sale racks and the brochure, which he still hadn't given her.

"Well, uh, not really. I guess. But it's as close as I could get on short notice."

"Life with you is going to be full of surprises, isn't it?"

"I'm not sure how to answer that."

"Then I have an answer for you. Yes, I do trust you. I trusted you then, but everything I saw told me otherwise. Then I checked your drink, just to prove that it wasn't what it looked like, but then it was. The facts were right in my hand. Even still, I wanted someone, anyone, to tell me you hadn't been drinking, despite overwhelming evidence. No one could. But now you have. I know you're telling the truth, and in a way that proves I'm not crazy after all. My heart was right. I'll never doubt you again." Her voice quieted. "Because I love you, and I won't ever not love you."

He reached up to cover her hand, pressing it gently but firmly into his cheek. "I want to do this right. Lacey, I love you with all my heart and soul. Will you love me, trust me and marry me, until death do us part?"

She glanced from side to side. "We've been lucky. You know someone is bound to come in any second now."

"I know. But I believe in miracles. Even small ones."

Lacey didn't back away. Instead, she sat gently on his bent leg, draped her arms around his neck and lowered her head until their lips were so close he could feel the heat. "I want to do this right, too. Yes, I'll marry you. Now give me a kiss," she whispered against his lips. "Make me see fireworks."

And he did.

* * * * *

Dear Reader,

Welcome once again to Faith Community Fellowship!

Often, when we get to know a person, we learn something that makes us wonder if we really knew them at all. Many people have things from their past they would like to keep buried, but when God calls, sometimes the painful lessons we learned can be used for His glory in mighty and meaningful ways.

Such is the case with Randy. If you've read the previous two books featuring Adrian and Bob, you've seen glimpses of the playful part of Randy's personality. But like most people, what we see on the surface doesn't always reflect who he is deep inside. It's hard to know what made someone the person we see today.

In the story, Randy used experience borne of old hurts and past wrongs to guide another person in his path to a better life, despite its difficulty. He had to put something else that was important, his growing relationship with Lacey, at risk. However, in the long run, the things we value most are the ones that withstand the bumps and difficulties.

I hope and pray that your hard lessons also can be used one day to ease someone else's burden. Even though it's often hard, it's worth it.

May God bless you in your daily journeys.

gail sattler

REQUEST YOUR FREE BOOKS!

2 FREE INSPIRATIONAL NOVELS
PLUS A
FREE
MYSTERY GIFT

Love Inspired.

YES! Please send me 2 FREE Love Inspired® novels and my FREE mystery gift. After receiving them, if I don't wish to receive any more books, I can return the shipping statement marked "cancel." If I don't cancel, I will receive 4 brand-new novels every month and be billed just $3.99 per book in the U.S., or $4.74 per book in Canada, plus 25¢ shipping and handling per book and applicable taxes, if any*. That's a savings of over 20% off the cover price! I understand that accepting the 2 free books and gift places me under no obligation to buy anything. I can always return a shipment and cancel at any time. Even if I never buy another book from Steeple Hill, the two free books and gift are mine to keep forever.

113 IDN D74R   313 IDN D743

Name	(PLEASE PRINT)	
Address		Apt.
City	State/Prov.	Zip/Postal Code

Signature (if under 18, a parent or guardian must sign)

Order online at www.LoveInspiredBooks.com

Or mail to Steeple Hill Reader Service™:

IN U.S.A.
3010 Walden Ave.
P.O. Box 1867
Buffalo, NY 14240-1867

IN CANADA
P.O. Box 609
Fort Erie, Ontario
L2A 5X3

Not valid to current Love Inspired subscribers.

Want to try two free books from another series?
Call 1-800-873-8635 or visit www.morefreebooks.com

* Terms and prices subject to change without notice. NY residents add applicable sales tax. Canadian residents will be charged applicable provincial taxes and GST. This offer is limited to one order per household. All orders subject to approval. Credit or debit balances in a customer's account(s) may be offset by any other outstanding balance owed by or to the customer.

LIREG05

TITLES AVAILABLE NEXT MONTH

Don't miss these four stories in March

WHEN DREAMS COME TRUE by Margaret Daley
The Ladies of Sweetwater Lake

Zoey Witherspoon got the shock of her life when her estranged husband showed up on her doorstep more than two years after he was presumed dead in a plane crash. Though thrilled that he was alive, Zoey struggled with giving her heart back to a man who had the power to break it all over again.

LESSONS FROM THE HEART by Dorothy Clark

When newspaper reporter David Carlson and literacy worker Erin Kelly teamed up for a story, there was an instant spark. But when Erin discovered David's lack of faith, their budding romance fizzled. David tried to move on, but when faced with adversity, would he find himself drawn back to Erin and her God?

A MATCH MADE IN BLISS by Diann Walker
Part of the BLISS VILLAGE miniseries

Lauren Romey needed a vacation, so her friends suggested a bed-and-breakfast. But when she wound up at the wrong one, she found herself in the middle of a contest staged by Garrett Cantrell's daughters—"Win Daddy's Heart." Lauren wasn't looking for romance, but Garrett's love was an appealing prize.

A FAMILY FOREVER by Brenda Coulter

When her fiancé was killed, pregnant Shelby Franklin feared she wouldn't be able to provide for her unborn child. The marriage of convenience proffered by the man who would have been her brother-in-law was her only choice. Tucker Sharpe had promised to look after Shelby, and he's determined to help her find love again—with him.

LICNM0206